One Day
and
One Amazing Morning
on
Orange Street

AMULET BOOKS
NEW YORK

ONE DAY AND ONE AMAZING MORNING ON ORANGE STREET

JOANNE ROCKLIN

Rocklin, Joanne.
One day and one amazing morning on Orange Street / by Joanne Rocklin.
p. cm.
Summary: The last remaining orange tree on a Southern California street brings together neighbors of all ages as they face their problems and anxieties, including the possibility that a mysterious stranger is a threat to their tree.
ISBN 978-0-8109-9719-6 (alk. paper)
[1. Neighborhoods—Fiction. 2. Trees—Fiction. 3. Oranges—Fiction. 4. Friendship—Fiction. 5. Family life—California—Fiction. 6. California—Fiction.] I. Title.
PZ7.R59Omm 2011
[Fic]—dc22
2010023452

Text copyright © 2011 Joanne Rocklin
Page 65: Prince Valiant comic strip reference from
Hal Foster: Prince of Illustrators/Father of the Adventure Strip,
by Brian M. Kane, Vanguard Productions, NJ: 2001. Page 96.

Book design by Maria T. Middleton

Printed and bound in U.S.A.
10 9 8 7 6 5 4 3 2 1

Amulet Books are available at special discounts when purchased in quantity for premiums and promotions as well as fundraising or educational use. Special editions can also be created to specification. For details, contact specialmarkets@abramsbooks.com or the address below.

ABRAMS
THE ART OF BOOKS SINCE 1949
115 West 18th Street
New York, NY 10011
www.abramsbooks.com

For

Arjun, Leo, Ravi,
and Rosie

The street I lived on was like a book
of stories, all different, but bound together.

—*The Memoirs of Ethel Finneymaker*

They all believed in magic,
but everyone's magic was different.

—*Stories and Lists of Formidable Words, by Ali Garcia*

MORNING

The Color Orange

I t was a hot summer day on Orange Street, one of those days that seem ordinary until you look back on it. Lawn sprinklers sparkled, mourning doves cooed, and the sky was an amazing blue, as it always was in L.A. Even at eight A.M., the sun looked like a giant egg yolk. In fact, a few parents made a joke about the sidewalk being hot enough to fry an egg on by noontime. One grumpy kid wondered aloud why anyone would be dumb enough to do that.

Everything seemed normal, except you couldn't help noticing the Day-Glo orange cone sitting at the curb in front of the empty lot. (The mysterious stranger didn't arrive until later.)

The empty lot belonged to the kids who lived on that particular block of Orange Street. They didn't have the papers to prove they were the owners, of course, but the lot had been theirs to play in ever since they could remember, which, even if you subtracted those baby years when nothing really sank in, was more or less a decade.

The lot had no house on it, but it wasn't completely empty because of its orange tree. Years ago, the tree had shaded the backyard of a house that was later torn down and never rebuilt. And oh, what a tree it was, with its juicy fruit and big huggable trunk and dark canopy of leaves! It even had a little plastic swing hanging from a big branch. The tree was the last living member of the grove that had given the street its name, long ago. Everyone knew that the coolest spot on the street (temperature–wise and otherwise) was under the orange tree. That's where the Girls With Long Hair Club conducted its meetings.

Over the years, hundreds of things had been buried under the lot's hard clay surface, whether by accident or on purpose. The mysterious stranger himself had come to dig up some small things, as well as something big.

Nasturtiums and sage and lavender grew all over the lot. They looked so grateful to be planted in the sun, you knew they would bloom forever. A huge, bushy bougainvillea vine climbed the lot's chain-link fence. Robert Green (302 Orange Street) liked to conduct his important, but lonely, missions behind that vine. He didn't pay attention to the orange cone because orange cones showed up on streets in Los Angeles all the time, and they usually meant street repair.

Bunny Perkins (308 Orange Street and a member of the GWLH Club) noticed the orange cone when she let her dog Ruff out, and went outdoors herself, to count snails. Summer always meant lots of fat snails—some could be found in the garden, others meandering across the sidewalks, leaving behind silvery, wet trails. Three snails on the front walk meant bad luck. Luckily, there were only two that day, an important point to note, especially on a morning when Bunny's mother was preparing to go on a trip by plane. Ruff ran to the lot next door and lifted his leg by the orange cone. Bunny phoned Leandra Jackson (301 Orange Street, another GWLH Club member) as soon as she could.

"What do you think that cone means?" Bunny asked.

"It's not the cone," said Leandra grumpily. Lots of things made Leandra grumpy lately, especially changes out of the blue. Or in this case, orange. "It's the color orange."

"Orange?"

"You heard me. In nature, orange means good things, like pumpkins, and juice, and autumn leaves, and sunsets. But when you paint something orange it usually means something not-so-good. Except, of course, if it's Halloween. And even Halloween is scary sometimes."

"It's summer."

"Exactly my point. So we're talking not-so-good. Like *danger*. Or *condemned*. And, of course, *keep out*."

"Keep out! I can't do that!" cried Bunny, her heart pounding. Bunny had lots of dependable ways to keep her mother safe, and one secret way involved climbing the orange tree. It worked every time.

"I'll call Ali right away," said Leandra. "I'll bet that cone means bad news. We're due for a club meeting anyway."

But Ali Garcia (305 Orange Street) wasn't worried at all. "Maybe it means an important person will be driving by, like the mayor," Ali said. "It could be something exciting. Maybe someone's going to make a movie about our street!" She and her little brother, Edgar, were sitting on the living room couch while they waited for Edgar's careperson to arrive. They lived right smack across the street from the lot and Ali had noticed the orange cone first thing that morning. "Actually, it looks just like a wizard's hat."

Leandra laughed, still grumpy. "Oh, grow up," she said. Leandra was five and a half months older than Ali, and often said that.

"Only kidding," said Ali. "See you soon."

It did look like a wizard's cap, thought Ali, staring at the cone across the street. When she had been younger, Ali had imagined the lot was a magical place, inhabited by witches, gnomes, fairies, goblins, wizards, etcetera, etcetera. Those creatures played tricks on ordinary mortals, terrified them, granted their hearts' desires, etcetera, etcetera, just as they did in all those great books she'd read.

The closest you got to real fairies in that lot were the tiny hummingbirds sipping nectar from flowers. Anyway, Ali was older now and considering a possible future career in science, probably paleontology, or archaeology. So she'd begun digging in the lot about two weeks ago, sort of as a summer hobby. She had always been curious about the true facts related to the property, which was sometimes provided by Ms. Snoops (303 Orange Street), the oldest living resident on the block.

Spread out on the coffee table were Ali's treasures from her most recent digs in the lot, not exactly the valuable treasures she'd discover on future digs in exotic places, but a good start: a jar top, two iron nails, a woolen sock. Ali's favorite was a little blue stone, shaped like a heart. It could be a wishing stone, if she still believed in that stuff.

Ali had also made a recent gruesome discovery. Ruff, Bunny's dog, had been digging holes in the lot, as usual, and that's how Ali had found the ancient cookie tin. The gruesome discovery was inside that tin: a head! It was a doll's head, not a human one, but still . . . Its face was cracked all over, its hair and one eyeball were missing, but it was still smiling faintly, despite its bad luck.

Ali put a few fingers in its poor little skull, making it dance for Edgar like a puppet.

"Hey, kid! What's your name? Will you play with me?" Ali asked, in a squeaky voice.

But Edgar didn't answer Ali's questions like he used to. He didn't ask his own questions, either. It used to be *"Why? Why? Why?"* all day long. And he used to say his name, and he knew all the letters of the alphabet and the names of a whole rainbow of colors. Even turquoise! Even fuchsia! And words. Lots of words! "So smart, and only two and a half years old," everyone used to say. Edgar himself would shout, "I'm *fart*!" And of course everyone would fall down laughing, Edgar laughing harder than everyone else. Just laughing and laughing and laughing. But Edgar's words and Edgar's laugh had disappeared ever since he'd gone into the hospital two months ago, returning home silent and pale.

Ali put the doll's head down. She touched the blue heart-shaped stone with the tip of her finger, then kissed her little brother.

"I wish for my heart's desire," she whispered.

Ms. Snoops (303 Orange Street) Reports a Murder

The kids called her Ms. Snoops because that's what she did. (Her real name was Ethel Finneymaker.)

That morning Ms. Snoops noticed the orange cone, too, when she went outdoors to deadhead her marigolds. She didn't like to disturb those hard-working 9-1-1 operators unless the situation was serious (especially so early in the day), but she knew that ominous orange cone could mean only one thing.

"Murder!" cried Ms. Snoops. She glanced around to make sure nobody had heard her, then hurried inside to make that early morning phone call.

On any other morning, if you happened to glance up at the

top corner window of 303 Orange Street, chances were you'd see Ms. Snoops looking at you as you strolled by. She'd give you an embarrassed wave, or a wink, or pretend to wipe some invisible dust specks from the windowpane. Then she'd go back to whatever she was doing before she started snooping.

The kids on Orange Street weren't exactly sure what that was.

Bunny worried that Ms. Snoops was a spy in disguise. (Well, a spy wearing a nightgown, or a shiny pink tracksuit.) She wondered if she should bring up that worry with her parents.

Leandra was positive that Ms. Snoops had committed a crime of some sort. Once she'd even seen a cop ringing Ms. Snoops's doorbell! She thought she'd glimpsed an electronic bracelet around Ms. Snoops's ankle on the day Ms. Snoops slipped on an avocado pit while taking a brisk stroll. The police were probably monitoring her activities.

Robert thought Ms. Snoops was a witch. He meant that in a good way. She had a thousand wrinkles that made her look wise, and she smelled of secret potions. Also, she'd recently lent him a book called *Incredible Magic Tricks for a Rainy Day*, which seemed to be the real deal, whatever the weather.

Ali knew Ms. Snoops the best, because she enjoyed

visiting her to discuss the history of Orange Street. But Ali kept changing her mind about Ms. Snoops.

Sometimes she thought

(1) Ms. Snoops, a retired schoolteacher, was amazingly smart, with one of those brains scientists liked to examine in their labs. Ms. Snoops was over eighty years old and had lived on Orange Street when it was part of a grove of trees. If Ali asked Ms. Snoops, "Who were all the people who've ever lived on Orange Street?" Ms. Snoops could reel off names, hobbies, what people liked to eat for breakfast—everything! Ms. Snoops also knew all the constellations, dog breeds, plant types, old movie stars, American presidents, and synonyms or antonyms for any word you threw at her.

On the other hand,

(2) sometimes Ali thought Ms. Snoops wasn't that smart. This was a surprising thought that occasionally flitted across her own brain and made her feel deeply ashamed.

But, then, she thought, maybe

(3) Ms. Snoops had a mysterious ailment which required rest, occasional exercise, and lots of vitamin C from orange juice.

Ms. Snoops did love her orange juice! She drank it at most meals, and sometimes, with a drop or two of sherry, just before she went to bed at night: certified, organic orange juice from the health food store. But after the February blossoms had bloomed and then the sun and winter rains had done their magic, Ms. Snoops got the sweetest most orangey juice for *free*, stolen from the orange tree growing in the lot across the street, with the help of her trusty, rusty fruit-picker pole.

Actually, it wasn't *stealing*. Ms. Snoops felt she had the same rights to the tree's fruit as the squirrels did. Who else took the time to personally clean up the dog poop and gum wrappers and cigarette butts around its trunk? Who else fertilized its roots or gave it long, cool drinks from a watering can? Or risked a strained back lugging a ladder across the street to hang some wind chimes, as well as a snazzy birdhouse (free with her Chicken McNuggets at McDonald's)? Ms. Snoops had many "rules of life," one of which was to help make her own neighborhood as nice as she could.

This included the prevention of murderous crimes. On this particular morning, she dialed 9-1-1.

"I'd like to report a murder," Ms. Snoops said, when the dispatcher picked up.

That wasn't exactly true, Ms. Snoops realized.

"Actually, it's an attempted murder I'm reporting."

That wasn't true, either.

"Well," Ms. Snoops continued, "the murder hasn't been attempted yet, but trust me, it will be attempted very, very soon!"

There was a short silence at the other end of the phone line, punctuated by static crackles.

"Madam, I'm afraid we need more information. How can you be certain of this murder-to-be?" asked the dispatcher.

Now Ms. Snoops was very confused. "Well. I—"

But how *could* she be so certain? What had made her call 9-1-1 in the first place? Ms. Snoops racked her brain, but she couldn't remember.

"I really don't know why I called. I'm so terribly, terribly sorry for disturbing you," said Ms. Snoops, and she hung up the phone.

"Mitzi, Mitzi," she murmured sadly. "My memory is disappearing again."

Ms. Snoops was talking to her cat, Mitzi, who was lounging on the windowsill. That was another of Ms. Snoops's rules of life: Always have a cat around to talk to. She figured if she didn't have a cat, she'd be talking to herself all day long, which would be unbearable. And all of her cats were named Mitzi, in honor of all the dear Mitzies who'd come before.

She hoped the children would come to the lot that morning. They always cheered her up. She looked out her window. Yes, there was that girl, Ali, the question-asker. How wonderful it felt to answer her questions!

Ali was talking to her little brother in his stroller. Ms. Snoops couldn't remember his name. And there was that young man—the little boy's nanny. And hiding behind the bougainvillea vine, she could see a boy, but could not recall his name (Steven? Charley? Hector?). She knew that pretty soon another girl would show up, the one with the animal name, and also the girl with the big hair. She couldn't remember their names either. So many kids had lived on Orange Street! How could she possibly remember all of their names?

But she used to remember: first names, middle names, last names, nicknames, wished-for names, and fun names-just-for-a-day. She could still remember some of the old ones. Agnes. Cricket. Gertrude. Larry. Pug. It was this new crop of kids whose names seemed to slip away from her, like wisps of smoke.

Now Ms. Snoops noticed the orange cone across the street, as if for the very first time that morning. "Strange," she said to Mitzi. "Must be repairing a sewer today."

She also noticed something else. Noises right beneath her front window! A car's engine was purring. A hand break was creaking. She opened her window and looked out.

"Maybe I have a visitor," she said hopefully to Mitzi, who took the opportunity to crawl out for a nice sunbath on the eave. "Now, wouldn't that just make my morning!"

A shadowy, mysterious figure was in the driver's seat, eating a sandwich. Actually, he was eating a hamburger and fries; Ms. Snoops could see that clearly now, especially with the binoculars she kept by the window for bird-watching. He was an ordinary-looking man (except for his bushy beard) wearing jeans, a floppy shirt, and a vest. She watched him take a bite of the hamburger. Then he put down the food, picked up a notebook, and began to write something.

Ms. Snoops had so many questions! What kind of person ate a hamburger and fries for breakfast? What was he writing? Should she call the police? But there was something else about that mysterious stranger. Ms. Snoops had seen him before. But where? When? Why, oh, why did he look so familiar?

Ms. Snoops sighed. It was time for her daily magic trick. She plopped down onto her yoga mat. Sometimes the trick worked its magic. Most of the time it didn't.

On the mat she placed a perfect orange that had been picked from high up on the south side of the orange tree, where the sweetest oranges grew. She sat cross-legged on the yoga mat in front of the perfect orange.

And then she chanted, over and over:

NOW, NOW
MAGIC *NOW,*
SHOW ME HOW,
MAGIC *NOW* . . .

Ms. Snoops figured if she could just keep noticing the oranginess of the orange and its sharp perfume and its pockmarks and its almost perfect roundness, then she could hold on to her disappearing memory. Remembering the distant past was a cinch—and something she loved to do! Worrying about the future was pretty easy, too. Remembering the recent past was much trickier, and lately she just couldn't seem to wrap her brain around lots of things happening right now.

But her stomach began to growl, and, oh, that orange smelled good! So Ms. Snoops stopped what she was doing to eat it for breakfast, with a nice hunk of Gouda cheese.

306 Orange Street, Which Was Actually the Empty Lot

Just around the time that car with the mysterious stranger pulled up under Ms. Snoops's window, Ali discovered her name spelled out in nasturtium seeds in the empty lot. Sitting cross-legged in a sunny spot near the fence, she just happened to glance down near her left foot, and there it was. ALI.

"Manny, look!" she called out to Edgar's nanny.

Ali examined the seeds again. OK, maybe the "A" was a bit of a stretch, but the "L" and the "I" did seem to be perfectly formed.

Manny was strapping Edgar into the orange tree's swing. "What's up?" he asked.

"Oh, nothing," said Ali. She sighed. She was being silly. What's the big deal about a bunch of straight lines? Any tidy squirrel or a particularly intelligent rat could have laid out the seeds like that. It was so hard to be a scientist when she kept hoping for miraculous things to happen.

Then again, strange and interesting things did seem to happen in the empty lot. For instance, the amazing ideas. Of course, you could get ideas anywhere, but Ali's best ones seemed to come to her in the empty lot. She had just had an amazing idea that morning, as a matter of fact, just before she discovered the nasturtium seeds. Ali couldn't wait to announce it to her fellow members of the Girls With Long Hair Club. She hoped they would agree that it was a kind and generous idea, the sort of idea that made you feel like a kinder and more generous person just for coming up with it.

But sometimes in the lot, someone would get an amazing idea, and soon after that, there would be an argument. Ali had some theories about why those two things would occur together. At that moment, she was considering two of them:

(1) There was a surplus of invisible, buzzing orangey electrons that inspired ideas and created friction, especially in warmer weather.

(2) Los Angeles was known as the City of Angels, and the

lot was a hangout for a group of bored, invisible angels, who liked to inspire ideas *and* stir up trouble.

The first theory sounded more scientific, but the second theory was more fun.

"Did you ever have a great idea that arrived out of nowhere, as if, say, a little angel whispered something in your ear? Something you'd known all along, but didn't know you knew?" she asked Manny.

"Lucky you," he said, gently pushing Edgar in his swing. "I have to work hard for my ideas, and they're not always so great."

Ali smiled at this, because in her opinion, Manny, as well as being politely modest, had very good ideas. His real name was Manuel but it had been so wonderful, so *fitting* when he'd said, "Hey, everybody, call me Manny the *Manny*!" Ali loved words, and she especially loved that words and names, like shoes, could *fit*.

Manny could juggle and do magic tricks. He entertained children in hospitals where he called himself Magic Manny. His torn jeans came from Planet One, the coolest store ever. He knew umpteen unusual things to do with an orange, such as piercing it with his penknife, inserting a straw in the hole, then drinking the juice *on the spot*! Today he had made a little rabbit for Edgar from a flattened-out orange rind. For all these reasons, Ali loved him.

And recently, about two weeks ago, just around the time Ali began her digging project, Manny had the best idea of all.

One morning during his first week at work as Edgar's nanny, Ali, Manny, and Edgar had gone to Pacific Park. Pacific Park was ten and a half blocks away. It had eight swings and a castle with turrets she could swoop down from with Edgar in her lap. They'd land in a big pile of sparkly sand.

Ten and a half blocks went by quickly when you were starting out and smelling the bacon and morning muffins at the diner, or hopping over a gas line at the pumps, or looking for TV stars sitting outside Starbucks. But it felt like twenty blocks going back home. Somehow the same sights weren't as interesting when you were seeing everything for the second time that day, all tired out. And nobody had looked like a TV star, going home.

But then, as they'd turned the corner onto Orange Street, Manny got his great idea.

"Whoa, now *that's* a tree for a swing," Manny had said, pointing to the orange tree, its thick branches like strong arms. As if they had a choice of other trees! The sycamore branches were too high to reach, and who ever heard of a baby swing on a scraggly old tropical palm?

Soon after that, Manny had bought Edgar's plastic swing with his very own earnings, a special, enclosed swing that looked like a little throne. And then Ms. Snoops hung up the wind chimes and that birdhouse from McDonald's, which Ali called the Birdhouse of the Golden Arches. Then Leandra got her own amazing idea for the Girls With Long Hair Club. And . . . presto! They had their very own private park and meeting place. Something happy had come about from something sad, although of course the sadness of Edgar's operation was much bigger than that happiness. But still.

Now, as Manny gently pushed Edgar in the swing, the bells on his dreadlocks tinkled and his skin smelled of patchouli oil. He pretended that the little orange-rind rabbit was pushing Edgar.

Ali stared at Edgar, hoping, hoping for a tiny smile. No dice. And then she remembered her idea, which was just too amazing to wait for the Girls With Long Hair Club.

"Manny, listen to my idea . . ." Ali began. But before she could finish, Leandra strolled into the lot.

"Whee-hoo! It's a scorcher already!" Leandra said.

Leandra flopped down under the big tree, her long hair spread out on the ground like a thick blanket. The goal of the club was to grow hair long enough to sit on. Leandra was almost at that goal, as she so often liked to tell the other club members. But it wasn't so obvious because her curly hair grew up, around, and sideways rather than straight down, like Ali's.

Edgar whimpered. Ali went over to him and put her hand on his warm little head, then kissed his fingers, one by one. Manny lifted Edgar out of the swing and gently bounced him on his knee in the shade of the tree.

"I wish Bunny would hurry up and get here," Ali said. "I have an idea I want to share."

"She's saying good-bye, and that will take her forever," said Leandra. "Her mother is going on a business trip by plane. What a baby."

"But—" Ali began.

"I know, I know," said Leandra.

They were silent for a few moments because they both understood. It was so hard for Bunny to say good-bye when her mother had to travel by airplane. Ali began to dig in the dirt with one of her archaeological tools (a garden trowel belonging to her dad). Ruff had already been digging there, too, and it was the same place she'd found the heart-shaped stone and the rusty nails. A fruitful spot.

"Well, let's discuss this orange cone business while we're waiting," said Leandra, grumpily.

"Maybe it means a marathon or a parade will be coming by today. That would be fun!" said Ali. "Why do we have to worry about something bad that hasn't even happened?" Especially when something bad already has, thought Ali, looking at silent Edgar on Manny's knee.

"I guess," said Leandra. "Hey, let's not even wait for Bunny. I have an idea I want to share, too!"

"You share yours, then I'll share mine." Ali felt that her own idea was so amazing it needed to go last.

But just then, as if out of nowhere, Robert appeared in the lot, from the direction of the bougainvillea vine. He was carrying a giant shoebox (NIKE, BLK+RD, 14w), which had once contained his father's sneakers.

"Hey, Rob-o!" said Manny. "How're you doing?"

Robert smiled broadly. He loved when Manny called him Rob-o! He wished other people would pick up on the nickname, but so far, no one had.

Leandra lifted up her head. "Do you mind? We're having a club meeting here!"

"So what?" said Robert, feeling his face flushing pink, like a grapefruit (Embarrassment Level One). "It's public property. Well, it's not public property, but *you* guys don't own it. And it's a free country, isn't it?"

Boy, did he sound like a jerk. *It's a free country?*, for halibut's sake! But he could remember a time, a few short years ago, when they'd all hung out in the lot together: selling orange juice to people walking by, putting on carnivals, launching imaginary rockets, or just doing nothing. Even doing nothing used to be fun! When exactly had things changed? He himself felt like the same person inside.

"Robert, how about giving us an hour or so?" Ali asked kindly. "Then the lot is all yours."

"Thanks," said Robert, "but I'd actually like to ask Manny a question."

"Fire away!" said Manny.

"One-on-one, privately," Robert said. Robert could feel his flushed face progressing to Embarrassment Level Two (tomato). And when exactly did his face start looking like some sort of produce whenever he was around these girls?

"Sorry, Rob-o. I'm working now," said Manny. "How about stopping by the Garcia's while Edgar's napping, say one P.M. or so?"

"Great," said Robert. Maybe his mission will have been accomplished by then. He shifted his big shoebox to his other arm, hoping one of the girls would ask him what was in it. Then he'd be able to answer, "Nothing. Yet." Heavy emphasis on the "yet." Just to keep them in suspense.

But nobody asked him anything. "See you later," said Robert, before slowly walking away.

"Now, where were we?" Leandra asked, glaring after him.

"Your great ideas," said Manny. He began to feed Edgar an orange slice. Edgar chewed it slowly, the juice dribbling down his chin.

"Right," Leandra said. "I was thinking—"

"Robert is lonely," Manny interrupted. "Maybe he wants to join your club."

Ali and Leandra giggled.

"Robert doesn't want to join the club. He just wants to eavesdrop, then make fun of us in front of my brothers. You should hear them go on and on," Leandra said.

"But really," said Manny. "I know the club is for girls with long hair, but maybe you could change your focus to include him."

"That's what I wanted to tell you. That's what *my* idea is

about. Changing our focus!" Ali said. "But not with Robert," she quickly added.

Manny began to push Edgar in the swing again. "How would you feel if your best friend suddenly moved to New Zealand?" he asked.

"Well, that's life," said Leandra, gruffly.

"Right. That's life," said Ali, feeling a twinge of guilt like a pinprick. That's exactly what her mother had said, but in a much kinder voice, on the awful day they'd told Ali about the tumor growing inside her brother's brain. In his cerebellum. *Cerebellum* was one fancy word she wished she'd never had to learn! "Why? Why? Why?" Ali had cried. "That's life, *mi vida*," her mother said. "It's nobody's fault."

Now Ali was afraid to look up and see Manny's disapproval, so she began busily digging in the dirt again.

After a while, Leandra said, "I'm not waiting for Bunny. Here's my idea."

Ali wasn't listening. Her trowel had dug deep, scooping up some more nails, and a small piece of charred wood. She put everything into her bag.

"Why do you bother with that junk?" Leandra asked.

"It's not junk," Ali said. "OK, maybe this stuff is junk, but it's fun to think I'll find something really important. And look at this find!" She took the little blue stone from the pocket of her shorts. "It's shaped just like a heart."

"Let's see," said Leandra, leaning closer. "Well, I think it's liver-shaped. Actually, no. It's shaped like a lung."

"Very funny," Ali said, frowning. She rubbed it again, then pressed the stone to her lips.

"I'll bet you're making a wish right now," said Leandra. "You are! You're actually making a wish."

Ali shrugged. "So what? It just felt like a wishing moment. I didn't want to waste it." She hurriedly dropped the stone back into her pocket.

"Oh, grow up!" said Leandra. "Anyway, back to my idea." She looked at Manny and twirled a lock of hair around her forefinger. "I think we should all have dreadlocks, like yours, Manny. I really like dreads, and then it will also be easier to see whose hair is the longest."

Manny grinned and made an OK sign with his thumb and finger, but Ali frowned. "That's not going to fit in with my own idea."

"Why not?" asked Leandra, looking annoyed.

So Ali told her about the imaginary, theoretical angel, and how the angel had whispered something that Ali had known, but just hadn't known she'd known all along: her amazingly kind and generous idea.

"Get to the point," said Leandra.

"OK, let's say we grow our hair so long we can sit on it. What's the good of sitting on our hair? So what? Then what will our club do?"

"Well . . ." said Leandra.

Ali continued. "But let's say we grow our hair really long, and then we *cut it off*! Then we can send it away to an organization that makes wigs for sick children who need them, like Edgar. I'm not saying Edgar should wear a wig. But lots of other children who've lost their hair would like to. And we would be growing our hair for a *reason*, to help other kids! It would be *altruistic*!"

A fancy, fitting word she was finally able to use.

"And our club could have another focus," Ali continued. "It could be the Girls Who Dig Club, for instance."

"You mean cut our hair *all* off?" asked Leandra, who had been thinking of a long, magnificent ponytail of dreadlocks with ribbons and tinkling silver bells threaded through it.

"That's the dumbest idea ever! And so is the Girls Who Dig Club!"

Ali caught her breath, tears springing from her eyes. "Well, I think the Girls With Long Hair Club is the dumbest idea ever!"

"It is not!" yelled Leandra. "And anyway, I wouldn't cut off my hair for *anybody*! Even Edgar!"

Invisible orangey electrons buzzed, or angels giggled, depending on your theory.

Edgar began to cry. Leandra stomped off. Manny shushed Edgar and put him gently into his stroller. He told Ali to cool down, hang loose, and schedule another meeting.

Soon the lot was empty, except for Robert–behind–the–vine again, still seeking to fulfill his secret mission.

Bunny Perkins,
308 Orange Street

Whenever her mother had to go on a business trip by plane, Bunny Perkins knew what she had to do. She chewed only on the right side of her mouth, tied her sneakers in double knots, and wore her mother's purple gardening hat outdoors, where she avoided sidewalk cracks. If she saw a squirrel or a hummingbird, she had to tap the hat, then blink rapidly three times. She also wished on a cloud (or weather permitting, the sun) at flight time. If school was out, she climbed the orange tree next door to actually touch the sky, then waved at her mother's plane for good luck. She always knew what time it was scheduled to fly by.

Her parents knew about the hat-wearing, which was

obvious. They thought that was kind of cute. Bunny didn't bother telling them about all the chewing and tapping and blinking and tree-climbing and sky-touching, which even she knew was less cute. But so far everything had worked, bringing her mother home safely every time. Bunny wasn't taking any chances.

And just before her mother went on a business trip, that's when the questions popped into Bunny's head: all sorts of questions about all sorts of things that needed to be answered right then and there, before her mother went away.

For instance, she had questions about her name. Her parents said "Bunny" was her real name, but maybe there was another name somewhere, a beautiful name that "Bunny" was short for.

"You know it says Bunny on your birth certificate," said Mrs. Perkins, as she packed her bag.

"But maybe you showed me the counterfeit one," she said, "and the real one is hidden away."

"You mean the one with *Rabbit* on it?" asked Mrs. Perkins.

Bunny tried to get a good look at her mother's nostrils, but her mother was bent over the blouse she was folding. Mrs. Perkins's sense of humor was the annoying kind, where it was hard to tell if she was cracking a joke. Unless you studied her nostrils. If her nostrils flared, that was a sign she was joking.

"You know, it's been nine whole years since we officially named you. I forget where we hid the real birth certificate," Mrs. Perkins said, zipping her carry-on.

Bunny leaned over and nostril-checked. "Stop joking," she said.

"Oh, honey, I'm sorry," Mrs. Perkins said. "I shouldn't be joking now." She hugged Bunny and squished Bunny's face against her chest. "You know you were named after a wonderful woman."

"Kids keep asking me if I eat a lot of carrots," Bunny said, in a squished-face voice. She felt her mother sighing.

"Maybe we made a mistake," her mother said.

Bunny had heard the story a zillion times about how she was named after someone from long ago whose name was Bunny. How her parents thought the name was just right because their Bunny was such a cute, perky "bunnikins" when she was born. She was a bunnikins all right, a soft, shivery, scared one. She couldn't imagine Leandra, for instance, letting anyone get away with making fun of her (not without punching them in the nose, or something).

Bunny didn't feel perky as she followed her mother down

the hall. She felt the way she always felt when her mother went on a trip by plane: slowed way down, like a turtle or a snail. But then another question occurred to her: Do turtles and snails ever feel perky, in their own way?

Before she could ask her mother that important question, Bunny's eye caught the eye of the wonderful woman she was named after. The wonderful woman was in a photograph hanging on a whole wall of photographs of dead and alive family members. The original Bunny Perkins was one of the dead ones. She had traveled from Missouri in a wagon train to a gold-mining town in California in the 1850s.

No one knew how the original Bunny had gotten her name. Modern-day Bunny's grandmother, Alice Perkins, had a wooden box with long-ago Bunny Perkins's journal inside of it. Not once did long-ago Bunny complain about her odd name in that journal. She had too many other things to think about, such as setting broken bones, delivering babies, smoking peace pipes with Native Americans, and cooking for her six children. Once, she met a roaring mountain lion by the creek near her cabin. She drew herself up as tall as she could, then hollered "AU–AU–AU–GUSTUS!" And that lion lumbered away, defeated. Later, she wrote in her journal, "*I am glad my dear husband Augustus's name sounds like a lion's roar! I daresay I quaked and trembled, but I did what I had to do, for all of our sakes."*

There was one thing modern-day Bunny knew for sure: Long-ago Bunny didn't look like she quaked. And she didn't look like a cute, perky bunnikins, either. She looked like she *shot* bunnikins, and skinned them and boiled them and gobbled them down in three or four bowls of rabbit stew at every meal, easy. She had a shotgun over her shoulder and she looked as tall as the bright pioneer sky. Her eyes were smart and squinty. Her mouth was a stern, familiar-looking straight line, like modern-day Grandpa Ed Perkins's mouth, just before he soaked his feet bunions in Epsom salts. That was probably because long-ago Bunny's feet were stuffed into skinny laced-up boots, peeking out from under her long skirt.

"I just figured out her real name," Bunny said grumpily. "It's Bunion. I'm named after someone named Bunion."

Mrs. Perkins laughed. "*Bunion* is a lovely name," she said.

Bunny was mad at herself for cracking a joke at such a serious moment, and mad at her mother for laughing, and mad at long-ago Bunny Perkins for being so brave, even though deep down, the wonderful woman was quaking like crazy. But Bunny knew what real quaking was like. You just couldn't hide it that easily, when you were a soft little bunnikins.

Ruff scampered to the front door, his tail going fast like a plane's propeller. Bunny let her dog outside. "I'll be there soon!" she called after him, knowing he was off to dig in the empty lot.

Ruff didn't seem to worry whether she'd be there with him or not. Suddenly, Bunny was mad at Ruff, too. Dogs didn't worry about *anything*! Not about plane crashes, or sad, sick kids like Edgar, or mean kids, or wars, or bad luck. Still, just for one day, just for one *minute*, Bunny wished she could be like Ruff, with no strong feelings about anything, except what was happening right then and there. Instead of worrying about the past and the present and the future, like she herself did, all in one quaking jumble.

Her father emerged from his dark, little office, his eyes smart and squinty in the bright morning light. His office used to be the kitchen pantry, but now it was where he spent hours telecommuting to work when Mrs. Perkins went on a business trip.

"How's my favorite nine-year-old?" asked Mr. Perkins, a joke which Bunny had heard a zillion times that year, so it wasn't really a joke anymore. And, according to her classmate Melissa Fung's aunt, if you counted the months you grew inside your mother's uterus, you were one year

older than everyone said you were, which made Bunny ten.
That was the Chinese custom anyway, which made a lot of
sense. Except that would add only nine months to your life,
which was something else Bunny would have liked to discuss
with her mother.

But at that moment Mrs. Perkins was telling Mr. Perkins
about all the carrot-eating questions from mean kids. To
Bunny's surprise, her father said, "Tell you what . . . You
think about what you'd like your new name to be, and when
Mom comes home, that's what we'll call you."

Bunny didn't need to think about it. She'd already
discussed the topic with Ali Garcia, who always had amazing
ideas. "I know the most fitting name," Ali had said. "Bonita!
A name that sounds pretty, and also means 'pretty.'"

"Bonita," said Bunny to her parents.

"Fine," said her mother, slipping on a crisp navy work
jacket.

Now would come the giant smooch between her parents,
then a kiss for her, and Mrs. Perkins would be out the door,
even though she had so many questions left to ask her mother.
Zillions of them.

For instance, why couldn't her mother just stay on the
ground and be a real estate agent and get to see the inside

of VIPs' homes, like Leandra Jackson's mother? And why couldn't the sky be the plain old sky like it used to be in pioneer Bunion Perkins's day, instead of a sky where bad things could happen?

But there was only time for two more questions.

"Do you think that orange cone means Danger or Keep Out?" Bunny asked.

"Neither, in my opinion," said her mother. "I wouldn't worry about it."

"Probably means No Parking for some reason or other," said her father. "Street cleaning, is my guess. Nothing to do with you and your friends."

And then the most important question of all. "What time is takeoff?"

"It's supposed to be eleven forty-five," Mrs. Perkins said. "Add a few more minutes and we'll be flying over Orange Street. I'll be waving."

"Me, too," said Bunny/Bonita.

Cone or no cone.

Bunny/Bonita Meets the Mysterious Stranger (Sort of)

It was the mysterious stranger's birthday. He leaned against his car and gulped down a bottle of water. After that, he began to whistle the birthday song to himself.

The funny thing was, it felt just like another morning, long ago, when he was ten and it was his birthday, that not-so-great birthday. The same sun heating up the oranges. The same heavy, still air in between the traffic noise. And the same . . . Holy moly! It was the same dog! The same cream-colored, foamy-mouthed, runaway Lab!

Of course it wasn't the man's dog, because the man's dog had been dead for quite a while. But for a second there, the stranger sure thought so, because everyone knows all good dogs are like all good dogs, and there was Ruff, jumping up on him, wagging his tail, loving him up.

And soon after that, there was Bunny/Bonita coming toward the empty lot. She was carrying a copy of *Little House on the Prairie*, which she loved because it took place in times before people traveled by plane, and wearing her father's watch. The watch was the old-fashioned kind with a loudly ticking second hand, to help her keep track of the passing time, so important on this particular morning. She had just finished tapping her purple hat twice and blinking six times as two squirrels scampered by, so the mysterious stranger startled Bunny/Bonita at a particularly vulnerable moment.

She saw Ruff prancing about across the street, even though he was trained to stay on one side of the street only! She saw the stranger feeding him a tempting delicacy. And then, suddenly, she stopped walking, because the strangest thing was happening to her. It was a blistering hot day, but her sneakers were trapped in a block of ice. RUFF, COME! HE'S A DOGNAPPER! Bunny/Bonita wanted to shout. But she discovered that her mouth was frozen shut, too. She just couldn't get it to work, to yell out LEANDRA! ALI! HELP! WHERE ARE YOU?

The man could have told her that everyone had gone off

every which way, in a big huff. (Except for one of them.) But he thought Bunny/Bonita looked like a girl who never talked to strangers, and he was right about that.

"Let's go, boy," the man said. He grabbed Ruff's collar and led him across the street, past the orange cone, and up onto the sidewalk to Ruff's stuck-to-the-spot owner. Bunny/Bonita suddenly became unthawed, hugged her dog, and escaped to the empty lot.

Then the mysterious stranger went back to his green car. He realized he was hankering for a big hunk of red velvet cake with vanilla frosting, or even better, a piece of boysenberry pie, and he was going to drive around town to find some. He'd return to the lot that afternoon, and maybe do some digging before it got dark.

Ruff, Under the Orange Tree

Orange trees need nitrogen. Store-bought organic fertilizer, the kind Ms. Snoops used, has nitrogen in it, and so does dog pee. Ms. Snoops wasn't exactly thinking about dog pee when she ate her breakfast orange with gusto. And Ruff didn't know he was keeping the orange tree healthy, when he did his business under the tree.

But Ruff knew so many other things, that morning:

He knew he was sleepy.

He knew the earth smelled of stinky fertilizer and worms.

It was warm under his nose, but cooler where his belly touched the ground.

Something tiny, maybe a ladybug, was tickling his left ear.

A small rat raced through the weeds.

Mitzi the cat was watching, somewhere.

Robert, eating a PB&J sandwich behind the vine, was watching, too.

Ants scurried over and under the hollowed-out orange skins.

A wasp buzzed above Ruff's head, but not close enough to sting.

A squirrel held her breath on the branch above the wasp.

Hummingbirds whirred and hovered, like tiny helicopters among the blossoms, feeding their babies again and again.

And above them all sat Bunny/Bonita, lost in her book, her wristwatch ticking.

And also Ruff was thirsty.

And he had to pee again.

And he was much too deliciously sleepy to get up.

All that, Ruff knew.

Here's what Bunny/Bonita would say: "Lucky Ruff, just lying there enjoying the here and now."

"The magic now," Ms. Snoops would say.

But they'd be wrong.

As he lay under the orange tree dozing, then waking,

then dozing again, Ruff, in his dog-smart way was also *remembering*:

the lamb bone deep under his right paw

the two and a half rawhide bones he kept burying and digging up again

the little teapot in the lot's middle, and beside it

that wooden thing with wheels he'd chewed in half

the stones of various shapes and sizes, buried and unburied, and the two glass marbles underneath

that jar with something in it, poking up from a freshly dug-up hole

And in every corner and all along the fence:

the peanuts, nasturtium seeds, raisins, smelling of rat and cat and squirrel

(some spelling someone's name, but this Ruff didn't know—he wasn't *that* smart!),

and of course,

those two moldy shoeboxes buried near the vines.

Ruff also remembered the green car, though the car looked grayish to Ruff. He remembered the person who smelled like food, who got out of his car to stare at the empty lot for a long time.

"Sit, Cream!" the man said, before he gave Ruff that bit of leftover hamburger meat. Then he said, "Good dog!" when Ruff did.

Ruff remembered the meat, salty and warm. He lay under the tree, hoping for more.

"All right, all right, you've made your point," Ms. Snoops would say, "Ruff remembers the recent past, much better than I do, as a matter of fact, but certainly not the distant past!"

Ms. Snoops would be wrong.

Didn't Ruff remember his mother, that black mutt with no name, and his father, the runaway hound? Didn't he remember sleeping in dark corners and shivering under the freeway? Foraging in garbage pails, the hunger squeezing his stomach? Didn't he remember the hard, cold cage at the pound, before the Perkins family brought him home, small and scared?

And what about those two moldy shoeboxes buried in the lot? Inside one, there was a tin of ashes and toys of that old cat Fluff. Inside the other, the bones of Moe the Macaw. One was a dear friend and one a dire enemy.

When Ruff yipped and yapped in his sleep, he was remembering all that.

Then Bunny/Bonita would probably pipe up loudly, "But you can't tell me Ruff worries about the future!"

Sure, Ruff didn't worry about his own future shoebox, or think about the poem Bunny/Bonita would one day place with his ashes:

The days are tough

Without my Ruff

We will miss you always.

(A poem similar to the one she wrote for her cat Fluff.)

But the near future, that's another story.

When that plane zoomed overhead and woke up Ruff at 11:50, and Bunny/Bonita whooped, "YOW-EE!" then reached up, touching the sky to save her mother, then clambered down from her branch, this is what Ruff knew:

He would lift his leg by the tree, and pee.

He would feel a whole lot better.

Then he and Bunny/Bonita would scamper home to 308 Orange Street, where his water bowl and his chew bone and his soft, odorous bed would be waiting.

Afternoon

M Is for?

While Edgar was having his afternoon nap, Ali brought some of her dug-up treasures over to Ms. Snoops's house. In her office, Ms. Snoops served orange-raspberry zinger tea and ambrosia, a delicious glop of orange slices mixed with coconut. Ali loved Ms. Snoops's sunny office, with its hundreds of books that lined the walls, the sweet-smelling bowl of potpourri of orange rinds and cloves on her desk and the comfy orange and green striped sofa with its lacy antimacassars to protect the sofa's arms from cat scratches. (Ali had learned *antimacassar* from Ms. Snoops, and so far it was the fanciest word she knew.) Sometimes it felt as if Ms. Snoops's office itself were the inside of an orange; it felt safe, and she didn't worry about Edgar as much while she was there. If she and Ms. Snoops were the same age, Ali knew they would be the best of friends.

"I had the most wonderful idea yesterday, while I was watering the tree in the empty lot," Ms. Snoops said.

"Yes! That happens to me all the time! It just happened this morning!" said Ali. "What was your idea?"

Ms. Snoops went to her desk and brought back a sheet of paper marked with a big handwritten "M." "As soon as I got the idea, I wrote this note to myself, just so I wouldn't forget. I'm embarrassed to tell you I can't remember what the 'M' is for."

"'M' is for mystery," said Ali, "but that doesn't help you much. How about muffins? Maybe you were thinking of baking your delicious orange muffins. You haven't made those in a while."

"No," said Ms. Snoops. "It was more important than that."

"Money? Medicine?" asked Ali.

"No, it had something to do with you, I believe."

"Me?"

"That's right, but I'm not sure how. Well, let's not let this spoil our get-together! What treasures have you brought this afternoon?"

From her bag, Ali pulled out the round metal disk, the icy-blue stone shaped like a heart, the iron nails, the woolen sock, and the rusty cookie tin with the head inside of it. She spread everything out on the coffee table.

Ms. Snoops placed the disk, the nails, and the sock in a separate pile. "These are common household items," she said. She picked up the scratched metal disk. "This is part of a glass preserve jar. Everyone put up fruits and vegetables in the old days. And if they were lucky to have orange trees in their yards, they made marmalade. I may be the only one around who still puts up her own preserves, however." She tapped on the iron nail. "A nail is just a nail. And the sock probably fell from an old-fashioned clothesline on a windy day. No particular memories come to mind about these articles. Hmmm . . . But *this* is interesting."

She held up the icy-blue stone. It twinkled in the sunlight from the window. "I would bet dollars to doughnuts this was one of Pug's stones. He collected unusual ones. That boy's pockets were so full of stones, sometimes his pants dragged. Pug would probably say this one looked like a heart."

"But it does!" said Ali. "Don't you think so?"

Ms. Snoops peered at the stone. "I guess you could say that," she said. "Funny little guy. He drew pictures, too, like his mother. His father didn't approve much of his artistry. He had an older brother who was good in sports, if my memory serves me."

"How nice that you remember all that," said Ali. "Sometimes I forget that other families once lived on this street."

"I used to love the old stories when I was your age," said Ms. Snoops. "I would pick up bits and pieces, do some digging, and fill in the holes myself, metaphorically speaking."

"That's just what I like to do!" said Ali.

"That's what all writers do when they create stories. They steal, disguise, and make things up."

"I'm actually planning on becoming an archeologist, not a writer," Ali said. Although she had to admit, sometimes making things up was a lot more fun than sticking to the facts.

"No reason you couldn't be both," said Ms. Snoops. "When I—"

Ms. Snoops stopped in mid-sentence. She reached for the rusty metal cookie tin. "What do we have here? Oh, my goodness! Can it be?" She opened the box slowly, then peered inside. "It is! It is! Shirley! Dear old Shirley! It's so good to see you again!"

She lovingly removed the head from the box and laid it in

her lap. The doll looked up at her with its one good eye, and its smile seemed to say, *Likewise, I'm sure.*

"I knew this doll when I was a young girl," murmured Ms. Snoops. "Oh, Shirley, the memories I have of you!"

Suddenly Ms. Snoops jumped from the couch, still clutching the doll's head. "That's it!" she cried. "Memories! 'M' is for memoirs! My wonderful idea was to write my memoirs! All these treasures you've shown me have brought back my memories, and I am so grateful."

"It's been a lot of fun," Ali said.

Ms. Snoops had begun to pace the room. "I will write down all my stories about Orange Street, before I forget them. And I'll add a brief history of orange trees, too. Did you know that citrus evolved at least twenty million years ago, near what became China? And then, eons later, the seeds and trees were carried by seamen to India where they called it *naranga* in Sanskrit. *Naranga!* Get it?"

"Orange!" said Ali.

"Right. And then the seeds were carried to Africa and the Mediterranean—" Here Ms. Snoops waved Shirley's head, presumably in that direction. "Where the Greeks thought oranges were golden apples and wrote exquisite poetry about their beauty, and so did the Roman poets and the Muslim poets and the European poets, you name it. And did you know they didn't even *eat* oranges long ago? They mostly loved the look of the tree and the wonderful smell of its blossoms. Sometimes they extracted oil from the fruit for an orangey perfume, or mixed powdered rind with hot water, a drink to soothe crying children. And they discovered lots of other useful things, for instance, that oranges cured scurvy. But not everyone realized you could just cut an orange into juicy chunks and have yourself a pretty good snack!"

"Really?" said Ali, very impressed. Ms. Snoops knew so much about everything, even an ordinary orange! "I wonder if I could give Edgar some powdered rind mixed with hot water when *he* cries," she said.

Ms. Snoops stopped her pacing. "Edgar? Who's Edgar?" she asked.

"My brother," said Ali, frowning. "You remember. He had an operation. He gets so cranky sometimes."

Ms. Snoops clapped a hand to her forehead. "Edgar, Edgar, of course I remember! How is he?"

Now Ali began to cry, her tears making tiny wet circles on the orange and green stripes of the couch. Ms. Snoops placed Shirley on the coffee table, then quickly sat down beside Ali, putting her arm around her.

"Edgar doesn't talk anymore. And he's so sad all the time," Ali said, leaning her head on Ms. Snoops's shoulder. "He just doesn't seem to be improving."

Ms. Snoops pulled a tissue from a box on the coffee table. "Sweetie, in today's modern world, there are much more effective medicines than orange rind," she said. "And our great friend time is the best medicine of all. If I could bottle it, and sell it, I'd be a billionaire. Ditto for love."

"I hope you're right," Ali said, blowing her nose into a citrusy-scented tissue. And then, because Ms. Snoops *was* a good friend (and how silly of her to think that age had anything to do with it!), Ali told her good friend about her own idea, her kind and generous idea, and how Leandra had said cutting their hair off to make wigs was dumb. Then Ms. Snoops told Ali about her old friend Gertrude, who used to live across the street from her at 306 Orange Street, where the empty lot was now. They'd had many, many disagreements over the years, all soon to be recorded in Ms. Snoops's memoirs.

Ms. Snoops held up the poor disfigured doll's head.

"Speaking of whom, Shirley was actually Gertrude's doll. Gertrude and I buried Shirley ourselves, or what was left of her. Because, as you can see, poor Shirley was belimbed."

"Belimbed?" Ali stared at the doll, whose faint, sweet smile now seemed to say, *I forgive you.*

"Not beheaded. Belimbed," said Ms. Snoops. "And believe it or not, I was blamed."

"Not you!" said Ali.

Gertrude Riggle,
306 Orange Street

Ms. Snoops spooned more ambrosia into each of their bowls.

"You know, my dear, you can live on the very same street and not know somebody very well at all. And that's why I want to tell you the story about me, and Gertrude, and poor old Shirley. And also, a backyard mule named Malcolm.

"We have to go way back to 1939, when I was nine years old. I remember so clearly the day I met Gertrude. I was looking out my front window and a dusty old rattletrap of a car with an Oklahoma license plate pulled up across the street. There was Gertrude, bouncing out of the car like a rubber ball, followed by an exhausted-looking man and woman.

Gertrude was carrying a doll. *She's too big to be carrying a doll*, I thought to myself. They all went into the Stott's house (306), which is now the empty lot. Next thing I knew, the exhausted-looking man and woman rushed outside again, got back into the car and drove off. And there was that girl sitting on the front steps, hugging her doll. Of course yours truly had to find out what was what!

"So I went over there. 'I'm Ethel,' I said. 'Who're you?'

"'Gertrude,' she said, holding out a grimy hand. 'I'm ten years old and I'm Mr. Stott's second cousin, once removed.'

"'Those your parents who left you?' I asked.

"She sat up straight and regal-like, pulling her faded and torn gingham dress over her knees, even bonier than mine. Then she smiled real wide, and her words came spilling out. 'Yes,' she said. 'They're off to have some exotic adventures in the Imperial Valley! How about that? Doesn't that sound grand?'

"I nodded, because it sure *did* sound grand. Imperial Valley! It was like they were off to the Land of Oz, or something.

"'Mr. and Mrs. Stott are very kind,' Gertrude continued. 'They don't have any children, so, lucky for them, I am available to be their adopted daughter for a while.' Gertrude looked down at her doll, which was naked and dirty and missing one eye. 'And I guess me and Shirley are lucky to be here, too, because the Stotts are rich. Very, very rich.'

"I was surprised to hear that the Stotts had been hankering for a daughter. They didn't seem like the parenting kind. Mr. Stott hardly talked to the neighbors, always puffing on a big, smelly cigar. Vain Mrs. Stott went around with her nose in the air and her hair in an up-do, just so. She ate ambrosia once a day, she told my mother, because she'd read somewhere it was the food of the gods, you see, and eating ambrosia would let her live forever. And they were always going off on far-away trips with their fancy pigskin luggage. Mr. Stott himself killed the hogs for that luggage. Well, that's what the kids on the street whispered to one another. I didn't know if it was true, but it sure gave me the willies, thinking of it.

"And the Stotts' new adopted daughter was just as stuck-up as they were. Whenever I saw her, she had something else to brag about.

"'Every day, practically, I get a new toy,' Gertrude told me. 'I keep them all in a big toy box in my bedroom. My bed is one of those four-poster kinds, with a giant canopy on top. And every night, practically, we eat roast beef and fancy desserts, with seconds, and even thirds, allowed. Lucky, lucky me!'

"We kids on the street didn't like stuck-up Gertrude much. We started singing a little song about her.

Shirley and Gertie, always-be-dirty!
Shirley and Gertie, never-be-purty!

"We called her Gertie, even though she kept insisting over and over that her name was Gertrude. Then she'd chase us around the block, trying to punch a nose or two.

"I guess I should have wondered why the Stotts didn't buy Gertrude a new doll or a new dress, or why she had dirt under her fingernails. Those questions never even entered my head.

"One day my mother heard us taunting Gertrude with that awful song. 'How very, very mean of you!' she cried, horrified. Let me tell you, my mother was formidable when she was horrified. (*Formidable* is a terrific word to know, by the way.)

"My parents sat me down for a talking-to. I told them we kids didn't like Gertrude much because of all the bragging about her lucky life with the Stotts, and also, her true parents' exotic adventures.

"My dad said, 'Exotic, my foot. Her parents are poor farmers driving south to California's border, to pick cotton and peas for pennies an hour. And sure, she's lucky! Lucky not to live with her parents in a tent in the mud, and fight for a sheet of toilet paper. And lucky to go to school in Los Angeles, and have enough to eat.'

"'I think it's time you learned the truth about Gertrude's life on Orange Street,' said my mother.

"And here's where Malcolm the mule comes into the story.

"Mr. and Mrs. Stott didn't have any children, but they did have this mule named Malcolm in their backyard. Mrs. Stott was crazy about Malcolm. She fed him candy, then brushed his teeth, and rubbed him daily with extract of rose petals.

"'My glorious chestnut Malcolm!' she exclaimed.

"An honest-to-goodness descendant of George Washington's mule herd, according to her. But to me, he was just a lazy old mud-brown mule, who'd lost his job to a tractor.

"The sad thing was, Mrs. Stott treated that mule better than Gertrude. She treated Gertrude like the servant girl she'd always wanted to have. There were no new toys or fancy desserts or four-poster beds; Gertrude had made that up. It was just 'Gertie, do this,' and 'Gertie, do that,' all day long. Washing windows and peeling carrots and ironing sheets and shoveling Malcolm's manure. Just like Cinderella!

"The day after my talking-to, my formidable mother marched across the street, had some words with the Stotts, and Gertrude got to come to our house for supper two times a week. And yours truly sure found out the truth about Gertrude's life. My formidable mother made me help Gertrude with her outside chores in the backyard, such as gathering fallen oranges, and hanging laundry, and shoveling up all that manure.

"Well, we became friends, Gertrude and I, believe it or not. At my house we played board games and made peanut brittle and played with my cat Mitzi. And after the chores at her house were done, we lolled around and read under the orange tree. Sometimes we pretended the tree was a magic theater, its leaves and blossoms a curtain, the ground around it a stage. We were chorus girls and cackling witches and princesses in faraway kingdoms. Gertrude's deepest wish was to be an actress. Then she could be Someone Else and Somewhere Else, you see. Under that tree, her wish came true.

"True, Gertrude was a pain. She was just the bossiest girl, and stubborn as a mule!

"Speaking of which.

"'Oh, that mule Malcolm,' Gertrude always said. 'Look at him giving me the evil eye!'

"If anyone was giving any evil eyes, it was Gertrude. Malcolm was the same old gentle Malcolm, smelling like roses, thinking everyone loved him like Mrs. Stott did. Not so. Gertrude hated Malcolm. She hated shoveling his manure every day, and she hated knowing she was loved less than a mule.

"One day we were in her backyard and Gertrude announced the cast for our next performance under the tree.

"'I'm Prince Valiant,' she said, waving an old curtain rod for a sword. 'You can be the fair Ilene, a damsel in distress. And Malcolm over there is my trusty steed.'

"Prince Valiant was a knight in a comic strip we loved. 'I want to be Prince Valiant this time,' I said. 'He gets to brandish the Singing Sword, and joust and kill ogres and fight crocodiles. Ilene isn't supposed to do anything except cry and beg him to be careful.

"'You're not right for the part,' said Gertrude. 'I have straight hair like Val. Your hair is too curly.'

"'But I can ride a horse!' I shouted. 'I ride my grandfather's horse on his farm every summer!'

"Gertrude looked like she was ready to pinch. 'Well, I rode horses on *our* farm!' she shouted back.

"We both looked over at Malcolm the mule, and I knew the idea hit us both at the same time.

"'Prove it,' I said. Of course, Malcolm wasn't a horse, but his mother was.

"'That's easy,' said Gertrude.

"She led Malcolm to the tree, climbed onto a branch, and hoisted herself onto Malcolm's back. Malcolm did a little shuffling around, and Gertrude said, 'See? I told you I can ride.'

"Malcolm circled around a few times, then suddenly reared up on his hind legs and let forth a sneeze like a geyser. And that's when he decided to buck. His limbs went in all directions at once. His head moved up and down and sideways, with his big ears flopping. GALUMPH, GALUMPH! Gertrude held on to his mane for dear life, bouncing up and down, baring her teeth just like Malcolm. He bucked a few more times, but mules aren't dumb. Malcolm finally understood that Gertrude would not be thrown. Gertrude was more determined than he was. He stopped bucking and stood still.

"'There!' said Gertrude, red-faced and panting. 'Now he

knows who's boss.' She jumped off the mule and said, 'Your turn.'

"'Forget it,' I said. 'You can be Valiant.'

"Gertrude grinned. 'Tell you what,' she said, 'you can be my helper knight.' She pointed to her doll lying propped up against the tree trunk. 'Shirley over there can be Ilene, the damsel in distress.' She brandished her curtain rod, and hollered, 'The terrible sword rises and falls! Hear my ringing battle cry: For Ilene!'

"Well, Shirley was a damsel in distress, all right. Malcolm ambled over to the tree, and next thing you knew we heard a loud *crunch*. That mule ate Shirley's leg! Gertrude screamed, but I was frozen to the spot, speechless. Malcolm munched his way through another leg, then the torso, then the arms. Gertrude kicked Shirley's head to safety, and threw herself on top of it, sobbing her valiant heart out.

"Malcolm brayed as if he were asking *Who did you say was the boss?* Then he washed down all that wood and glue with an orange for dessert.

"Now Gertrude gave *me* the evil eye. 'It's all your fault, Ethel!' she cried. 'If you'd only let me be Prince Valiant in the first place! Your fault! Your fault!'

"She didn't talk to me for a few days. I still had to help

her with her chores, though. I missed being friends. One afternoon, I apologized, even though it was Malcolm's fault, too. And Gertrude's, for riding Malcolm so hard. I even gave her Patsy, one of my favorite dolls, cleaner than Shirley used to be.

"'I'm really too old for a doll,' Gertrude said, but she took Patsy anyway.

"Then we lovingly placed Shirley, or Shirley's head, in a cookie tin, and gave her the dignified funeral she deserved."

Ms. Snoops took a sip of her orange-raspberry zinger tea. "And guess what? Gertrude's wish eventually came true!"

"She became an actress?" Ali asked.

"Well, no. But one sunny morning that rattletrap of a car came clattering up Orange Street. Her parents had found better jobs working in a shipyard, and they'd come to pick her up and take her Somewhere Else, just like she'd wished. And she never let anyone call her Gertie, ever again." Ms. Snoops sighed. "Oh, that girl was a pain! Fun, though, and I grew to love her. Our friendship has been infrangible."

Leandra was fun, too, when she wasn't being a pain. Ali had to admit she even liked the Girls With Long Hair Club, except for its focus on long hair. "What's infrangible?" Ali asked.

"Go look it up." Ms. Snoops pointed to her giant dictionary across the room. "*Infrangible* is an important word to know, especially where friendship is concerned. And remember, as hard as we try, and it's so very, very important to try, you can't know everything that's going on behind people's front doors, or in their hearts and minds."

"I wish we could," said Ali.

Leandra Jackson,
301 and 301½ Orange Street

I t was so hot on Orange Street that afternoon, you could practically see steam rising up from the sidewalks. Even if your side of the street had the afternoon shade, as Leandra's did, that wasn't really an advantage, temperature-wise. It was a good idea to stay inside for a while until the day cooled down.

That was fine with Leandra. All she felt like doing, really, was sitting around and complaining in her grandparents' living room. Her grandparents, Big Mom and Little Pop (301½ Orange Street), lived in a one-room apartment with a bathroom, built on top of the garage attached to Leandra's house.

Big Mom and Little Pop had made the apartment cozy and cheerful. The walls of the sleeping section were painted Sea Breezy Blue and the living room and eating section Jasmine Pink and the cooking section was painted Hot Banana. The bathroom was Sail Away Green. Every chair had a plump pillow for the crook of your back and a footstool to put your feet on. Their home was always the right temperature for sitting around and complaining; toasty warm on chilly days, or deliciously cool in summer because of a giant, squeaky fan on the ceiling. In a corner was a big golden birdcage with a sign that said 301¹⁄₁₆ ORANGE STREET, inside of which was an old African Grey parrot named Nelson, who could talk. (He also sang "All You Need Is Love" every evening as the sun went down.)

Big Mom was tall, with soft flesh on her arms that wriggled like pudding. Little Pop was short in stature, but muscular and strong. Even so, Leandra was worried about him. That's because Little Pop had once had a heart attack. He had a tiny pacemaker (which Little Pop called his "battery") deep inside his chest. Seventy-five early morning push-ups helped keep that battery running, Little Pop said. And while he exercised, he and Nelson could sing "Dem Bones" straight through, without missing a single beat. Leandra sometimes did push-ups with Little Pop. After a while she could sing "Dem Bones" straight through, too.

The foot bone connected to the leg-bone,
The leg bone connected to the knee bone,
The knee bone connected to the thigh bone,
The thigh bone connected to the back bone,
The back bone connected to the neck bone
The neck bone connected to the head bone
Now hear the word of the Lord!

"Whee-hoo!" said Little Pop when he got to the end of the whole song.

"Whee-hoo!" squawked Nelson.

The best part about being at 301½ was that Big Mom and Little Pop listened to every word Leandra said, even when they were all in the middle of an exciting card game.

"It's funny that our girl lives on Orange Street," said Big Mom to Little Pop.

"I know what you mean," said Little Pop. They often knew what the other meant when no one else did. "Go fish."

"Whee-hoo! Game over!" Nelson squawked again. Everyone ignored him.

Leandra had been talking about that morning's argument with Ali, as well as complaining about the usual things such as her parents, her brothers, and the Blessed Event.

"Leandra herself is like an orange isn't she?" Big Mama gave her husband a poke in the ribs and reached for a card. "Tough on the outside, but inside—"

"She's sweet," said Little Pup. "And tart. But still sweet." And he winked.

"Do you have any queens?" asked Leandra.

"Go fish," said Big Mom.

"Fish! Game over!" squawked Nelson.

True, Leandra felt sweet when she was in 301½. But everywhere else, lately, she mostly thought of herself in lemony terms, like *sour*.

That's because Leandra's mother was going to have a baby. (The Blessed Event, in her grandparents' words.) Leandra thought that was one of the most embarrassing things ever to happen to their family. It was fine for a mom to be pregnant when her other children were infants, all hanging out together cluelessly in double- or triple-wide strollers, but it was a different story entirely when one of those children was nine, and the nine-year-old's twin brothers, P.J. and A.J., were eleven. And all of them totally understood

(1) how it happened and

(2) what their family was in for.

"Maybe you should have consulted us . . . before," Leandra had said to her parents, the day they had announced the news, months ago. A big ruckus erupted and P.J. and A.J. rolled around on the kitchen floor, giggling wildly. Because of what that "before" implied.

"We thought you'd be as thrilled as we are," said Mrs. Jackson. Their father stood grinning by her side. They were holding hands, which was also embarrassing.

"Thrilled? Uh, no–o," said Leandra. "Here's why: Babies poop in their diapers. They also spit up."

The giggling from the kitchen floor increased in volume as Leandra continued to describe the serious truth of the situation. "And because of all that, babies stink. They yell, day in and day out. Slimy drool hangs down from their chins. They take over all the rooms with their stuff. They sit in their car seats throwing Cheerios. And all they have to do is take one teeny–weeny step, or smear junk in their hair, or pick their little wet noses, and out comes the camera. Big deal."

Mr. and Mrs. Jackson laughed annoyingly, as if Leandra were exaggerating.

Leandra thought she knew a thing or two about babies.

She'd watched enough of them being pushed up and down the neighborhood streets in their thrones on wheels, or lugged around on their parents' backs or chests. She'd observed them bawling their heads off over nothing, or laughing their heads off over their own private jokes. The parents themselves often had dark circles under their eyes.

In the videos of Leandra when she was a baby, her parents, too, had dark circles under their eyes. Although Leandra had to admit she herself had looked very adorable with those mashed lima beans in her hair. Then her hair grew longer, up, around and sideways, just like her mother's. The two of them had loved to brush and braid each other's hair. And they'd been talking about dreadlocks, which would have been the very next step.

But one day, just like that, her mother had cut her hair very short. "To save time," she explained. Now Leandra understood where that saved time would be going.

And then there was poor little Edgar Garcia. He had acted just like all those other babies, before he got sick and very quiet. That was another thing. That was a very important thing. Babies got sick and everyone worried about them like crazy.

A.J. came up for air from the floor. "How many are in there, anyway?" he asked.

"Only one," said Mrs. Jackson.

"And it's a girl," said Mr. Jackson. "Now our family will have two girls and two boys. Even Steven." Leandra's father looked proud of himself, as if he'd planned it that way.

Leandra had an almost-happy thought, though it was tinged with jealousy around the edges.

"So you'll be quitting your job?" she had asked optimistically. It would be fun to have a full-time-at-home-mother, even though that full-time-at-home-mother would probably spend a lot of time doing laundry and breast-pumping and taking care of the baby.

"Oh, no," said her mother. "I don't want to do that. But we're going to need lots of help with the house and you kids."

"A nanny!" Leandra had exclaimed.

Leandra thought it would be fun to have a cool nanny like one of those ladies you read about in books, with a British accent and lots of fairy tales to tell.

"No," said Mr. Jackson. "Nannies can be expensive. Luckily, we have other options."

The "other options" were Big Mom and Little Pop. They weren't British and they weren't really nannies, but they were cool in their own way. As soon as they and Nelson were settled in, Big Mom and Little Pop introduced the System. Little Pop said he'd learned the System in the Wars, although he didn't say which wars, or where, or when. Big Mom seemed to have been there, too, because she knew exactly how the System worked.

"See this?" Big Mom had pointed inside a medium-sized Macy's shopping bag.

The three Jackson kids peered into the bag, which was overflowing with a bunch of greasy playing cards.

"Left over from the Wars," explained Little Pop, which didn't explain anything at all.

But Big Mom continued, "Every time you kids do something positive, like get a nice note from your teacher with compliments, or clean Nelson's cage, or even make your bed in the morning, you'll get one of these cards. The better the deed, the higher the card, decided by Little Pop and me. And we'll keep your cards in your own cookie tin right under our bed."

"When you get enough points, you can cash them in for some pretty good stuff," said Little Pop.

"Like what?" asked P.J.

"Oh, dollar bills, bubble gum, sneakers, whatever," said Big Mom.

"Sounds good to me," said A.J.

"Sounds like bribery to me," said Leandra.

"Not at all," said Big Mom. "Because if you do something not-so-good, like punching, teasing, or running around like a pack of wild coyotes, we'll take a card out of your cookie tin and throw it right back into the shopping bag."

And the best part of the System was that you weren't penalized if you occasionally admitted to some random imperfect behavior, just sitting around 301½, playing a game of cards. And that *did* make you feel a bit sweeter inside.

"So I yelled at Ali and now she's mad at me," Leandra said, then told her grandparents about Ali's idea. "I said her idea was dumb and that I wouldn't cut off my hair for anybody, even poor little Edgar. Any sevens?"

With a frown, Big Mom handed over three sevens.

"Fish!" said Leandra, displaying her hand.

"Whee-hoo! Fish! Game over!" squawked Nelson.

Little Pop gathered up the cards for another game. His fancy shuffling made a tall fountain of cards.

"It's the yelling that concerns me," said Big Mom. "Maybe a quiet discussion would have worked better."

"That reminds me of something," said Little Pop. "Do you remember the Yelling Contests?"

"Of course!" said Big Mom. "They were a big problem."

"What Yelling Contests?" asked Leandra.

"When you were a very little girl, Adam John or Phillip John would yell into your crib to see how many seconds it took to wake you up. The next day the other twin would try to break that record."

Big Mom called A.J. and P.J. by their full names because she thought the initials were silly. "Why have names in the first place if you didn't use them?" she'd say.

Little Pop shuffled twice more: another fountain of cards, then a quick show-off ripple behind his back. "Remember the Pip?" he asked.

Big Mom rolled her eyes. Just in case Leandra didn't know the story (she did), Big Mom told it again.

"You were three when you accidentally swallowed that orange pip, which is another name for seed, as you know. The boys told you a tree would begin growing inside your belly if you drank anything. For two whole days you refused any liquid, and to get you to drink something (anything!), your mama told you orange pips wouldn't grow in chocolate milkshakes. So you drank chocolate milkshakes for two days, until we assured you the pip had passed. No milkshakes for the twins, of course."

"You had to feel sorry for those boys," said Little Pop. He began to deal the cards. "Changes are hard."

"I guess," said Leandra.

"But look at them now. Practically model citizens!" said Big Mom. "It's the System, of course."

"But what about the snails? That was only a week ago," Leandra reminded them.

A.J. and P.J. had each plopped a snail into Leandra's tomato soup at dinner. They insisted the snails had already died of natural causes, but that prank cost them quite a few playing cards.

"As I said, changes are hard," said Little Pop. Suddenly, Little Pop laid down his cards, his hands shaking. Beads of sweat appeared on his forehead. "Heat's getting to me," he said softly.

Leandra jumped up to bring Little Pop a glass of water and a cool, damp towel from the Hot Banana kitchen. She wiped her grandfather's forehead. Then she ran to bring him a footstool from across the room.

"Better?" asked Leandra anxiously.

"Better?" asked Nelson, with a small, worried squawk.

"Much better," said Little Pop. "Game on."

Big Mom gave Leandra her special, piercing look. The look said *I'm about to ask you a question, but I already know the answer.* Leandra began to deal the cards.

"This is what I want to know," said Big Mom, putting her big hand on Leandra's, so that the dealing was interrupted. "Here's this girl, OK, a grumpy girl, tough on the outside, but inside, so scared of that baby coming down the pike."

"Whee–hoo!" said Little Pop. "Man, is she ever scared. What's the real reason for *that?*"

"I'm not scared about anything! Well, maybe just a bit," Leandra said.

"Give us the reason," said Big Mom. "Come on, let's hear it."

There were actually two reasons. One was obvious, and one was scary—black–magic scary.

"I'm not so sweet inside," Leandra said, looking down at the cards on the table.

"You think we don't know that?" said Big Mom. "We said *tart* and sweet. Like an orange." Suddenly Big Mom stood up from the table, arms akimbo, flesh wiggling.

"Look at me! Do you think I was always seventy-two years old? Don't you think I know what it feels like to be a preteen, hormones popping around inside, moods blowing every which way like the wind?"

"Whee–hoo!" said Little Pop. "And pretty as a princess!"

Leandra looked up. Actually, it was hard to imagine Big Mom as a preteen and pretty as a princess, no matter how hard she tried. Big Mom was, well, Big Mom. "I'm going to be a terrible older sibling. It runs in the family," she said. "I wish with all my heart I could be a good one, but I don't think I can be."

"Oh, baloney! What you're feeling is normal," said Little Pop.

"That baby will be lucky to have you," said Big Mom.

"I guess," said Leandra.

Big Mom's eyes narrowed. "Is that all?"

Leandra studied her fingernails. "That's all," she lied. She couldn't tell them the other reason. She didn't even want to think about that one.

"OK then. A few other things," said Big Mom. "Your hair could actually lose a few inches, in my opinion. And do you really want to sit around all summer with two old fogies?"

Leandra did feel less lemony, all of a sudden, she had to admit. A lot less. "I have to go make some phone calls," she said.

An Angel and Robert Also Visit Ms. Snoops, and Robert Hifflesnuffles

Ali loved Ms. Snoops's giant-sized *Oxford English Dictionary*—the *OED*, as those in the know called it, which now included Ali. The *OED* was so big it stood on its very own wooden podium by the window in Ms. Snoops's office. You needed a magnifying glass to read the tiny type on its thousands of pages.

"Take your time, dear. And I hope your friendships turn out to be as infrangible as mine and Gertrude's," said Ms. Snoops, who was curled up on her window seat, happy to have someone else to talk to besides a cat.

Ali slowly turned the almost see-through pages, blinking at all the delicious words she found on the way to infrangible:

Ignoble. Imbonity. Imperiwiggle. Incandescent. Infallible. Infossous.

"Something strange happened this morning," Ms. Snoops murmured.

Ali was so engrossed in the wonderful words, she didn't hear Ms. Snoops at first.

"So strange, so strange," repeated Ms. Snoops.

Now Ali looked up at her friend.

"I was gazing out my front window, minding my own business," Ms. Snoops continued, "and, in front of my house, someone was sitting in a green car. It was olive colored. Or maybe sea-green, or a shade close to emerald. I'm not really sure . . ." Ms. Snoops's voice trailed off, and her forehead was wrinkled in concentration.

"So what happened?" asked Ali.

"What do you mean?"

"You were talking about a green car," Ali said.

"I was?"

"Yes, and someone sitting in it."

Ms. Snoops clasped her hands tightly to her chest, as if she were trying to hold on to something. "Oh, right! It was a ghost," she said.

"A ghost?" Ali felt a stirring, as if one of those invisible, theoretical angels from the empty lot, having accidentally fallen asleep on her shoulder, was beginning to wake up.

"Yes. Someone who has been dead for many, many years."

Ali couldn't think of anything to say to that. The invisible, theoretical angel opened one eye.

Ms. Snoops giggled. "Then, just before the *ghost* drove away in his green car, I got a better look. And I realized it must have been the slant of the sun, or his bushy beard, or my mind playing a trick on me, reminding me of someone who used to live on Orange Street, years ago."

Ms. Snoops had made finger quotes around the word "ghost." Ali's little angel yawned and went back to sleep. Ali herself sighed with relief because, for a second or two, she'd thought Ms. Snoops was a bit crazy, talking about ghosts. Ms. Snoops had so many thousands of memories, decades' and decades' worth! It was only natural they'd get in each other's way.

Ali went back to the *OED*. There it was. Infrangible.

Infrangible, in-fran'gi-ble, adj. Not capable of—

"Is that your friend Leandra, with her dog?" Ms. Snoops asked suddenly. "Or is that the girl with the animal name? I can never remember who is who."

Ali ran to the window to look. "That's Bunny. She's the one with the dog."

It was puzzling to Ali why Ms. Snoops couldn't seem to remember who was who, when the who's were so different. If you were comparing Bunny and Leandra, Bunny would be a little breeze, and Leandra would be a blustery, hot Santa Ana wind. Or Bunny would be a whistled tune under your breath, and Leandra would be a marching song, or the loud music they always play during the TV commercials.

Ali opened the window, leaned out, and called, "Hey!"

Robert poked his head out from behind the bougainvillea bush.

"Not you, Robert! I was talking to Bunny," Ali shouted, even though she knew that was *ignoble* of her. "Bunny! The meeting was cancelled!"

Then, to Ali's joy, there was Leandra herself, strolling down Orange Street toward the empty lot! Leandra looked up and waved at Ali. "Come on down," said Leandra. "We'll have another meeting!"

In the meantime, Robert had raced across the street, carrying his big shoebox. He loped up Ms. Snoops's outside and inside stairs, two at a time, and burst into her sunny office.

"What are *you* doing here?" Robert asked Ali, panting a little. Robert was a boy some people called chubby. In any case, he wasn't used to loping up anybody's outside and inside stairs, two at a time.

"I guess I should ask you the same question," said Ali. "*I'm* looking up a word at the moment."

"Which word?" asked Robert.

"Specifically, infrangible," said Ali, returning to the *OED*.

Infrangible, in-fran´gi-ble, adj. Not capable of being broken or separated into parts.

"Then I guess I'm here to do that, too," said Robert.

"Oh, sure you are," said Ali, without looking up. "*Which* word, then?"

Robert glanced around the room a bit wildly, his ears pinkening (Embarrassment Level One: grapefruit). He couldn't think of a word as interesting as Ali's at that moment, so he made one up. "Hifflesnuffle, for starters," he said. Looking at the size of Ms. Snoops's dictionary (a dictionary that needed its own table, for halibut's sake!), Robert gambled that *hifflesnuffle* was in there, somewhere.

"I'll bet that's not even a real word. But here, be my guest," Ali said, handing him the magnifying glass.

Robert stepped up to the podium. He slowly turned the

thin pages of the *OED*. "Well, if hifflesnuffle's not in here, I can always look it up online."

"Remember, if you can't find it, that doesn't mean it's not a real word," said Ms. Snoops. "New words get invented every day. That's why the *OED* is so voluminous."

Actually, when you came right down to the truth, neither Robert, Ali, nor Ms. Snoops needed a dictionary or a computer to tell them what hifflesnuffle meant. Ali had had a sudden insight, which may have had something to do with Robert's pink ears.

Hifflesnuffle: hif–ul–snuful (v.) –snuffled, –snuffling, –snuffles. (tr). To like someone when that someone doesn't like you back.

"What's in the shoebox?" Ali asked kindly.

Robert looked up from the *OED*, startled. "Shoebox?"

There she was. *Wow, oh, wow,* thought Robert. The old Ali! His former orange juice–selling business partner, his fellow astronaut in space, on whom his very life had once depended, standing right in front of him, as if she'd never gone away.

"That one," said Ali, pointing to the big shoebox on the floor by the dictionary stand. "What's in it?"

"Oh, nothing," said Robert. "Nothing, *yet.*"

"OK." said Ali, shrugging. And *poof*! The old Ali disappeared into thin air, right before Robert's eyes.

Maybe a hint of magic would impress her, since she was always wowed by Magic Manny's stuff, Robert thought. He put down the magnifying glass. "By the way," he said to Ms. Snoops, "you know that book you lent me? Do you mind if I keep it for a while longer?"

"Which book?" asked Ms. Snoops.

"You know, *Incredible Magic Tricks for a Rainy Day.* It's really great."

Oops, thought Robert. Ms. Snoops was pretending she didn't know what he was talking about! He shouldn't have brought it up. Maybe the book was so special, Ms. Snoops wanted to keep it a secret, sort of like a pact between the two of them.

"Oh, is that a book of mine? Sure, keep it as long as you like," Ms. Snoops said.

"Thanks," said Robert, and winked.

Ms. Snoops smiled and winked back.

Ali hurriedly gathered up her treasures from the coffee table. "I have to go now," she said. "Leandra and I have something to discuss, and soon Edgar will be waking up from his nap and asking for me." Oh, how she wished *that* was true!

Then Ms. Snoops said something that made Ali's sleeping

invisible, theoretical angel suddenly awaken—and sit up straight.

"Who's Edgar?" Ms. Snoops asked.

The invisible, theoretical angel began whispering furiously in Ali's ear, and Ali realized something she'd known all along, but hadn't really known she'd known. The thought made her sit down slowly on Ms. Snoops's orange and green striped sofa.

Ms. Snoops's memory, whispered the angel, was like the lacy antimacassars on the orange and green striped sofa's arms. Ms. Snoops's memory had little holes in it, here and there, where facts slipped through and disappeared: people's names, titles of books, answers to questions Ms. Snoops had to keep asking, over and over. But then there were the parts of her memory with no holes at all—those would make her memoirs grow fatter and fatter . . . all those stories, all those historical and scientific facts she knew, all those wonderful words she remembered. *Naranga! Infrangible!* It was so confusing, and so, so sad.

Now it was Ali's turn to hug Ms. Snoops.

"Edgar is my little brother," Ali said. "But I promise I'll be back soon, to read those memoirs you were going to write. I'll help you remember."

"That would be lovely," said Ms. Snoops. "And a nap sounds likes a good idea right about now."

"I guess I'll go now, too," said Robert. "May I please borrow your fruit-picker pole? I'd like to pick some more of the oranges, the ones you said were extra-special." He winked at Ms. Snoops again.

"I'll give you some of mine! No need to pick them yourself," said Ms. Snoops, winking back at him. She filled a paper bag for both Robert and Ali from a big bowl of oranges on her coffee table. "These are the tree's sweetest oranges," she said. "The perfect ones that were hanging from its topmost, southerly branches." And then she added, "Personally picked by me. This old body can still scamper up a ladder when it wants to!"

After they'd gone, Ms. Snoops watched the two of them from her window. Ali looked up at her and blew a kiss. Robert hifflesnuffled behind Ali, off to his meeting with Manny.

"This has been my lucky day," said Ms. Snoops. "Two guests!"

Manny Has the Answer

Robert sat down beside Manny on the front steps to Ali's house.

"What's in the shoebox?" Manny asked.

"Nothing," said Robert. And there wouldn't be, not today anyway, because his secret mission hadn't worked out as he'd planned. He let out a long sigh, but it was a satisfied one. Ali wasn't home, but it still felt good to be there. Just like old times, long ago. Well, not so long ago, maybe two or three years back. They used to sit on those same stairs and count the seconds between the lightning and the thunder, to calculate how far away the storm was (five seconds = one mile), not even caring if they got soaked. Or they'd cheer on the L.A. Marathon. Small stuff, babyish stuff even. But satisfying.

"So. What's on your mind, Rob-o?" asked Manny.

He actually did feel like a Rob-o, sitting there, talking one-on-one with Manny. "I'm into magic, as you may or may not know. Like yourself."

"Good stuff," said Manny.

"And, well, I was wondering if you'd give me a pointer or two. Basically, not to put too fine a point on it, I mean, for starters—" Robert pulled up one of his socks, then another, waiting for the right words to come to mind.

"Go on," Manny said. The great thing about Manny was that he listened. He *really* listened. His brown eyes never once left your face.

"Like how do you do it?" Robert asked. "No, I don't mean that, exactly. What I mean is, how do you *wow* them? I haven't had much success . . . yet."

Actually, he'd mostly failed in the wowing department. Except for that one trick he'd performed, for his mom. But moms, in general, were incredibly easy to wow.

Manny continued to stare.

"How do you do it?" Robert repeated.

"Yeah, Rob-o, I heard you," said Manny, slowly. "I'm thinking hard right now. It's an important question and I want to come up with the best answer."

Suddenly Manny straddled the railing of the porch, then landed gracefully on the front lawn. "As a matter of fact, your question is so important, I think it calls for some *po-eh-tree*! Listen carefully, now!"

He did a pretty good moonwalk, some more fancy footwork, some power moves, and then began waving his finger and moving his head to the rhythm of his words:

"You find a doozy of a trick and you do it for a crowd,
Be choosy 'bout the trick if you want them to be WOWED
You gotta find it
Hear me? FIND it!

"You repeat that trick 'til you see it in your sleep
You gotta beat that trick 'fore you take it to the STREET
That means practice
Hear me? PRACTICE!

"When you're set for the show, you gotta stay in the NOW
Just forget about Rob-o! Yes! That's how,

Just forget him
Y'hear? FORGET HIM!
Yeah!"

Manny leaped onto the stairs again. "That's my answer," he said.

"It is?" asked Robert.

"Lighten up, man! And think about your audience."

"I *do* think about my audience. All the time, every single second!" cried Robert, suddenly feeling very un-Rob-o-ish. "My audience is a great big hundred-pound gorilla that's ready to tear my head off!"

Manny stared at him again, and he looked as if he were about to come up with some more answers (maybe some answers Robert *understood*, for mackerel's sake!) when there was a soft, plaintive wail from inside the house. Manny ran inside, and after a short while he returned, carrying a flushed and sleepy-eyed Edgar, just up from his nap.

"When you're set for the show, you gotta stay in the now," Manny crooned.

This time Manny's poem sounded like a lullaby. Edgar put his head on Manny's chest. "We're off to the lot. It's cooler there. Come with us?"

"I'll pass . . . for now," Robert said.

And so it happened that everyone was in the empty lot that afternoon (except for Robert, who had gone home to practice —the only pointer from Manny which seemed to make any sense!).

Just around the time Mitzi decided to pounce.

Cat Behind the Nasturtiums, Waiting

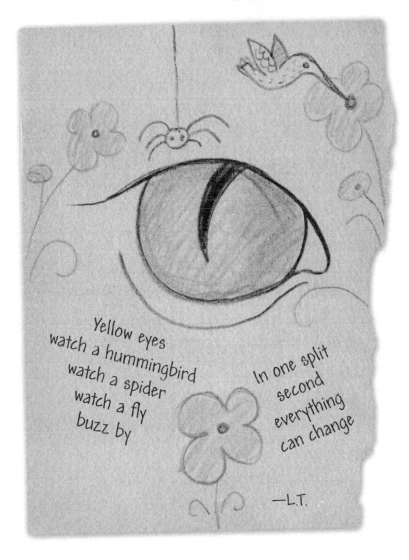

Yellow eyes
watch a hummingbird
watch a spider
watch a fly
buzz by

In one split
second
everything
can change

—L.T.

On Top of the Birdhouse
of the Golden Arches

Much later, they'd all discuss how so much had happened in one small space and one small space of time that afternoon in the empty lot. Mitzi the cat didn't pounce right away. A few other things happened first. Things having to do with *words.* There were:

(1) Ali's new word,

(2) Edgar's strange words, and

(3) all those mysterious words on those scraps of paper in the old glass jar.

So when Mitzi burst from her silent hiding place behind the jumble of orange nasturtiums, raced up the tree, then made her long, graceful leap, no one was able to stop her in time. That's because everyone had been distracted by the meaning (and mystery) of all those words.

Ali's word was *infrangible,* the word she'd heard from Ms. Snoops and examined further in the OED. A word she'd never expected to use so soon! Leandra had just apologized for yelling and saying mean things.

"I accept your apology," said Ali, linking arms with both Leandra and Bunny/Bonita. "We are infrangible."

"What's that?" asked Leandra suspiciously, who wasn't sure if infrangible was complimentary. To her it sounded too much like a fruit gone bad.

"I mean our *friendship* is infrangible," said Ali. "That means unbreakable. We've been friends since we hung out in our strollers together. And we'll be friends until college when we'll probably move away to different cities. And even then we can still chat online and get together during vacations. That's what Ms. Snoops does with her old friend Gertrude."

Bunny/Bonita nodded her head. "Sticks and stones can break your bones, eggcetera." Although, not exactly, thought Bunny/Bonita, since the eggcetera part was how words could never hurt you. But words *could* and they *did.* It was a bit confusing.

Bunny/Bonita was glad the club was infrangible anyway.

Ali lifted Edgar from his stroller. "And I'll check on your idea about smaller wigs, Leandra," Ali said. "Maybe you won't have to cut off more than a few inches."

A soft fuzz of brown hair covered Edgar's head but you could still see his ziggidy-zagged scar. Edgar had been wearing a baseball cap that said angels, but he'd pulled it off. The little red hat was lying in the deep mulch under the tree, where, Ali supposed, a little wig would lie, too, if he'd been wearing one and pulled it off. She couldn't imagine that kids' wigs were glued on. What a sad thought.

But now Manny had begun to juggle and it was hard to have sad thoughts when Manny was juggling. Two balls were golden, two were silver, one was bright fire-engine red. Manny always asked everyone to keep their eyes on the red one to help him concentrate, and before Ali knew it, her sad thoughts were juggled away. She put her little brother into his swing.

And then, as she pushed Edgar back and forth, something amazing happened.

Maybe it was the musty coolness under the tree's leaves, or the juggling, or maybe it was because Ali was pushing the swing higher than usual. All of a sudden, Edgar said, "Ahhh," very softly.

And he said it again. "Ahhh."

That is to say, Ali and Leandra heard "Ahhh."

Bunny/Bonita heard "Bahhh," or "Buhhh."

"He's saying my name!" Bunny/Bonita whispered.

"*Your* name? He's saying *my* name!" Ali whispered back. "*I'm* his sister!"

"Actually," said Leandra, "he's saying the back end of *my* name."

"He is not!" said Ali and Bunny/Bonita at the same time.

"Eeeeh," said Edgar.

"See? *My* name!" cried the three girls, forgetting about the infrangibility of friendship.

"Stop arguing!" cried Manny. "Edgar said *something*. That's what's important now."

The girls had never seen Manny angry. It was as if it had suddenly begun to rain, after one hundred days of L.A. sunshine. They were so surprised, for a few seconds none of them could think of anything to say.

Manny grabbed the chains of the swing and looked into Edgar's eyes. "Say it again, little guy." He spoke in a soft, calm voice.

"Whatever it was . . ." whispered Bunny/Bonita.

"Please," said Ali. "*Please.*" She fingered the little stone heart in the pocket of her jeans.

But Edgar just stared straight ahead. Then he put his thumb into his mouth, as if to block any more sounds from coming out. Ali could feel her eyes smarting. She didn't want to cry in front of her brother.

"Let's have some oranges," Ali said, rummaging in the bag from Ms. Snoops. "These are from the very, very top of our tree, a gift from Ms. Snoops." Manny pierced the tops with his penknife, then gave them straws to draw up the golden juice. He even did the same for Edgar. When the fruit was sucked dry, the girls ate the pulp. The pulp got between their teeth, looking gross, and that was funny, but when they put the skins over their teeth, that was even funnier, even though they'd done it a zillion times before. And then they lay, infrangibly, under the tree.

"Those oranges are refreshing on a day like today," said a deep voice.

Startled, the girls turned and saw a man standing at the entrance to the lot. He must have been standing there for a while, watching them. (He'd actually been watching them all day.)

Ali and Bunny/Bonita sat up and looked anxiously at Manny. But Leandra said, "They're from our tree. The sweetest ones are way on top."

"Leandra!" said Bunny/Bonita. She realized it was the same man she'd seen acting much too friendly with Ruff that morning. Of course, Leandra wasn't afraid of anything, but still, you didn't talk to strangers just like that. The man *looked* strange, too, with his thick beard and vest and clunky hiking boots, on a hot day meant for sandals. He was bald, but he seemed like a man who shaved off all his hair on purpose; a man who would never think of wearing a wig, for any reason. He had a thick drawing pad under his arm.

"*Your* tree?" said the man, with a smile.

Ali felt nervous but she also felt like giggling. It occurred to her that it was upside-down to have a shiny bald head and a bushy beard. And then she wondered why the man had said *those oranges ARE refreshing* instead of *those oranges MUST BE refreshing*, as if he'd already been tasting them himself. She decided he must be a person who sleeps in his car and when he's hungry, forages for food. "It's OK," Ali said kindly, "there are plenty of oranges to go around. You can pick some."

But Manny was frowning. "Can I help you?" he asked.

The man came closer. He flipped open his drawing pad. "I

was just sketching the Valencia over there," he said, nodding toward the orange tree.

He'd drawn the tree in pencil. Its oranges were small, white balls, like ornaments. Its leaves were a lacy, gray swirl. Bunny/Bonita wished she could draw like that! Leandra wondered why the man needed to draw the tree at all, when a digital camera could do a clearer and more colorful job. And Ali thought the tree was prettier in real life, although, until that very moment, she hadn't realized how lovely the tree actually was. It was as if the drawing itself was whispering, *Take another look.*

Manny stepped in front of the children. "I'm not sure I like it that you're drawing us, man," he said.

You had to look closely but, sure enough, around the drawing's tree trunk were the shaded outlines of four people. And a tiny, blurry person in the tree's swing.

"Here, it's yours," said the man, ripping the page from his pad. He handed the drawing to Manny.

While all this had been going on, Ruff had been digging furiously in the same spot Ali had found the heart-shaped stone.

The man took in a sharp breath, and said, "Your dog has found something."

He strode to the far end of the lot where Ruff had dug his hole. Ali, Leandra, and Bunny/Bonita followed. The man bent down to pull up an old half-buried glass jar. Ali could see that it had a rusty disk on the top, just like the disk she'd shown Ms. Snoops, which meant it was from an old preserve jar. The man put down his drawing pad and unscrewed the jar's rusted cap, twisting it hard with his hand.

"Well . . ." the man said, looking inside. He whistled a soft melody to himself, a melody the kids didn't recognize. Then he reached in and pulled something from the jar. They saw that it was some folded-up paper, which the man carefully unfolded and separated into two pieces. The pieces tore as he did this, but he read them anyway. That took him a long time. When he was done, tucking the jar under his arm, he folded the papers together again, creasing the edges gently with his thumb and finger. He put the paper into the jar, screwed the cap on tightly, and dropped the jar back into Ruff's hole. Then he bent down and raked the earth around the jar with his hands.

"There was something else in this hole," he said, looking at the kids, "buried on top of the jar. Did any of you kids find it?"

Ali was looking down at her sneakers. She had her hand in her pocket. The heart-shaped stone felt warm and smooth. She really wanted to keep it.

"Maybe the dog—" the man began. Ali looked up at him, but didn't say anything. The man gave a little shrug and walked slowly from the lot. Ali grabbed an orange and ran after him.

"Wait," she said, handing him the fruit. "An orange *is* refreshing on a day like today."

"Thanks," said the man. He put the orange into the big side pocket of his vest. He was smiling, but Ali thought she saw tears in his eyes.

"The lady across the street told me about you," Ali said. "You used to collect stones when you were a boy, right?" She reached into her pocket and showed him the heart-shaped stone. "Then this is yours. I was pretending it was my wishing stone."

The man took the stone, turning it over and over in his palm. He glanced quickly at Ms. Snoops's house, and shook his head. "Nope. Not mine," he said. He didn't look as if he wanted to say more. Then he gave back the stone, holding Ali's hand for a second in both of his. "But keep wishing."

"Thank you. I will," said Ali, and she ran back into the lot.

Leandra was already opening the jar. The others crowded around her as she pulled out the scraps of paper.

Was it someone's last will and testament?

Someone dead and buried, but very, very rich?

Was it a map to buried treasure? (Buried *right there in the lot!*) Would the man be back to dig for it in the dead of night?

Was it a note from someone in danger? Was it a love letter from long ago?

Nobody asked these questions out loud, but it was as if they'd floated right out of that old jar, along with the pieces of paper.

What was actually on that paper was something none of them expected:

Nothing at all.

The scraps of paper were blank, more or less. True, there were splotches and water marks and mud drops on them. And if you squinted a bit you could see what looked like an upper case "D" and a wiggly lowercase "Y." (Maybe.) But there was nothing that would have made the man's eyes go back and forth and up and down, as if he were reading something. It was all very disappointing.

"That man was just a weirdo," said Leandra.

But Ali and Bunny/Bonita and Leandra, and even Manny holding Edgar in his arms, continued to stare hard at the pieces of paper, as if hoping the invisible letters would reappear, if they waited long enough.

That's why nobody was prepared for what happened next. The air was hot and still, but suddenly the wind chimes were clanging like crazy, leaves shuddered, and branches snapped.

Mitzi had made her move.

While everyone studied the mysterious note, Mitzi scrambled up the tree's trunk, then leaped on top of the Birdhouse of the Golden Arches. She swung there precariously for a split second as her prey fell to the ground, followed by Mitzi herself.

Everyone ran to the tree. Ali grabbed the cat by the scruff of her neck, dropped her at the far side of the lot, then raced back to where everyone else was crouching down in a circle, examining Mitzi's prey—if prey was the right word.

"It's a jelly bean," said Bunny/Bonita.

But the wrinkled brown being had a tiny beak. Its eyes were closed and it was breathing very fast.

"It's not a jelly bean, silly," said Leandra. "Look. Its tiny heart is beating. I think it's some kind of bird."

"Poor little thing," said Ali.

Manny was standing above them, Edgar asleep again on his shoulder. "That's a baby hummingbird, fallen from its little nest on top of the birdhouse," he said.

A hummingbird! Bunny/Bonita took a big breath, tapped her purple hat, then blinked three times.

"Where's the mother?" Ali asked.

"She must be here, somewhere," Manny said. "If not, she'll be looking for her baby when she returns."

They all looked at the orange tree. Its leaves were still and silent. The Birdhouse of the Golden Arches was still swaying slightly, a little speck of a nest, smaller than a walnut, perched on its roof.

"But meanwhile, the mother's baby could die!" said Bunny/Bonita.

"One of us should take it home and nurse it back to health," said Ali.

"Oh, no! Not me! Sorry. I can't take that bird home," said Bunny/Bonita, thinking of all the hat-tapping and eye-blinking that would be required until her own mother returned home safely.

"Neither can I," said Leandra. "Nope. Impossible." She could feel that black-magicky fear again, making her heart tighten up like a fist.

"Then it's settled," said Ali. "Manny and I will take it home. But first we'll go straight to the library for some hummingbird books." A semi-amazing idea occurred to her. "This could be a new focus of the Girls With Long Hair Club. Birds! We could be the Girls Who Save Birds' Lives Club." It was only a semi-amazing idea because there wouldn't always be birds to save. But there was this poor, tiny bird now. And that was a start.

"I think it would be better to phone a wild bird expert," said Leandra. She looked down at the hummingbird. Maybe she didn't have to worry so much. It was such a teeny tiny bird. Just a bird! Maybe that black-magicky stuff didn't count with birds.

Her heart opened up, and a question flew out. *What will you call it?* Teeny? Little Hum? Bean? "I've changed my mind," Leandra said. "We know something about birds at our house, so *I'll* take it home."

"Well, I want it, too," said Ali. "Let's have a vote."

Leandra almost yelled, but she decided not to. She pulled a wrinkled tissue from the pocket of her shorts, then gingerly placed the bird on the tissue. "There's no time for a vote. I was the one who called the meeting, and now I'm adjourning it!" She hugged Bean gently to her chest, and for the second time that day, Leandra raced from the lot.

Robert Green,
302 Orange Street

While all this was going on in the empty lot, Robert Green was sitting on the bottom bunk of his bed, trying to juggle some tennis balls. He was also thinking about the three biggest secrets of his life; three secrets that were connected, like the big metal rings of Manny's Magic Ring Trick.

Secret Number One was a little mouse named Harry Houdini. The day before, Robert had captured him in the empty lot at dusk. He'd made a comfy hotel for Harry out of another shoebox of his dad's (MEN'S SANDAL, BWN, 14W), which was hidden under the bed. The shoebox was padded with cotton balls and sprinkled here and there with tempting trail mix and salami. But Harry Houdini didn't appreciate his new home much, if at all. All night long the lonely mouse squeaked to be let out, and Robert figured that a companion mouse would calm him down. So Robert's mission had been to find a suitable friend for Harry. He had been trying and trying since early morning, but no dice.

Robert leaned down to peek under the box's lid. As usual, Harry exploded from the box and raced around the bedroom, every now and then leaping in and out of an open drawer. Finally, Harry Houdini shimmied up the pole of the bunk bed to the top bunk, exhausted.

Robert tossed one ball into the air, followed by another ball, then watched both balls bounce across the floor. Juggling was so impossibly hard! He could hear Harry scratching at the blankets above him. Sighing, Robert put aside his third ball and climbed the bunk bed ladder to grab the mouse.

Green likes mice.

That's what kids would say if they could see him now. Even though he'd mouse-napped Harry Houdini from the empty lot strictly for training purposes, luring him into the shoebox with treats.

"Hey, little guy," Robert said, gently stroking Harry's

mushroom-colored body. "Don't you want to be the star of the show?"

Apparently not, because Harry Houdini wriggled free again, sliding down the pole to hide under Robert's pillow.

Secret Number Two was the *true* answer to the question, "How can I get my tricks to work and wow an audience like you do?" He had just discovered the answer a short while ago that afternoon, on his own. And Robert found it odd that Manny hadn't mentioned it, and recited that poetry stuff instead. It was as if Manny wanted to keep the secret all to himself. Robert hadn't figured Manny to be that kind of guy.

The *true* answer to his question about wowing an audience, and the real reason for Manny's success, was something Robert had learned online. It was on the website where Magic Manny shopped, with its snazzy eye-popping demo videos and expensive props.

"Sure, anyone can wow an audience," Robert said to Harry Houdini, whose pointy ears were now emerging from under the pillow. "All you need are big bucks!"

Robert liked the sound of the sneer in his voice. He sounded cooler with a sneer.

To be fair, Manny himself didn't really deserve that sneer. Manny didn't buy the biggest buck items. His Bending Key

Trick? $24.95. His Cigarette Up-Your-Nose Trick? $14.95. His Gravity-Defying Juggling Balls? $19.95. His Magic Ring Trick was the most expensive, at $32.50.

Then again, it all added up to more bucks than, he, Rob-o, could afford. But Manny was older, and a working man.

When he, Rob-o, was a working man, he'd spring for the incredibly expensive tricks. He couldn't wait to see the look on everyone's faces when he was able to master some of those incredibly expensive tricks.

Especially Ali's face.

That was Secret Number Three. That look on Ali's face was something Robert wished for in the deepest pocket of his heart—the look on Ali's face when she was with Manny, as if Manny were some sort of superhero or something! Or the look on her face when she was taking care of her little brother, like Edgar was someone she'd jump into a lake for, or walk a trillion miles for in a Walkathon. Real love, man. Ali was the neatest, kindest person on Orange Street. (Almost as kind as the old Ali used to be.) If Ali looked at him like that, then that would mean, he, Rob-o, was pretty neat, too.

Sure, maybe he'd been acting not so neat lately. Maybe like a jerk, for starters.

"He's exhibiting a bit of an emotional developmental lag," Mr. Pokrass, the principal, had told his mother.

True, he'd showed up late once or twice, and lost one or two library books, and disappeared into the boys' bathroom to eat chocolate bars a couple of times. Lots of eleven-year-olds were emotional laggers (like Leandra's brothers, for starters).

And so it wasn't really his fault, and even if it was, there were some good reasons for his own particular lags. Because, speaking of disappearing, everything seemed to be disappearing on Orange Street lately, and that was getting him pretty down.

Life had been going along very well when all of a sudden his best friend Nick (309 Orange Street, now for sale) disappeared to New Zealand. Robert hadn't heard one word from Nick yet, even though he'd had so many sleepovers in Robert's top bunk, and he loved fish and computers and werewolf tales as much as Robert did. Nick, whom Robert had taught to make his trademark shark face, a dazzling virtuoso display of lip-curling and teeth-baring. Audiences (well, only the two of them, so far) roared with laughter at that shark face and Robert thought that Nick could have been his magic show assistant, or even his *partner*, for halibut's sake, if he'd hung around. But now Nick was too busy kayaking and hunting and fishing (or whatever you did in the wilds of New Zealand) to even bother e-mailing him. Robert had so many questions to ask his friend. Like, ha, ha, where's Old Zealand, for starters?

Harry Houdini dashed under the bed. Robert hung face-down over the side and watched the mouse select a sunflower seed from the shoebox.

"Sure, New Zealand is far away, but that's a lame excuse, right, Harry? Because the Internet is everywhere!"

Robert noticed that his voice sounded deeper and more gravelly when his head was hanging down like that. "The Internet is *everywhere*, man!" he repeated, louder this time.

There was a soft knock at his door. "Are you all right?" his mother asked.

"I'm fine," said Robert. Just as Harry was making another run for it, Robert grabbed him and placed him under his quilt. The plan had been to introduce the mouse to his mother after a training period. Harry wasn't ready yet.

Mrs. Green opened the door a crack and peeked in. "Are you sure you're all right?"

Maybe he'd stop acting so babyish if his mother stopped

treating him like a baby! Like asking him if he was all right, over and over.

Robert lay across his quilt casually, his right arm on top of the mouse underneath. The quilt had colorful fish on it. Robert's entire bedroom, in fact, was done up in an aquatic theme. He even had splashy aquamarine waves painted on his walls. Harry Houdini's wriggling made the quilt's fish look as if they were swimming upstream.

Mrs. Green didn't seem to notice. "Your father will be here to pick you up soon," she said.

"I can tell time, Mom," Robert said. He waved his left arm, the one with his wristwatch, hoping to distract his mother from the job of his other arm. That's what magicians learn to do—distract the audience from the magician's trickery. Then, as a guaranteed distraction, he flashed a modified shark face at her.

His mother took a deep breath. Robert could tell she wanted to tell him he was being snippy, but she decided not to.

"Just wanted to remind you," was all she said. "Your father doesn't like to wait."

That was another thing. Life had been going along pretty well until "Dad," as Robert's mom used to call him, got that new name: "your father." Talk about disappearing! Sure his father came to get him every Wednesday evening and alternate weekends. But his shaving stuff and his clothes and his books and his camera and his paintbrushes (it was his dad who had painted the splashy waves on his wall) and Dad himself, with his deep, gravelly voice and big feet had—poof!—vanished from 302 Orange Street, just around the time Robert had started acting like a jerk.

It wasn't as if he were the only jerk doing stuff on Orange Street—making fun of girls, hiding stink bombs in garbage pails, talking snippy to adults . . . for starters. He was just the newest jerk. If Leandra's brothers were bad influences, was that his fault? And hadn't he been a voice of reason, that time A.J. Jackson, wearing a Superman cape, wanted to use a dog leash to swing from his grandparents' ceiling fan? (Although those guys had been acting less jerky lately, for some unknown reason.)

And then, all of a sudden you had a little kid like Edgar disappearing into the hospital and coming out all different: no smiling, no talking, and he was just a little kid, man! It could happen to anyone, of course, but why Edgar, for mackerel's sake? Edgar, who was too tiny, and let's face it, too sweet, to even think about acting like a jerk!

When you came right down to it, that's what Robert loved about magic tricks. It was all about disappearing and reappearing, disappearing and reappearing. And the disappearing and reappearing part happened when *you*, the magician, wanted it to happen!

Now Robert stood in front of his dresser mirror, wearing a towel as a cape, and a sneer. "It's time, ladies and gents, for The Great Rob-o's Incredibly Expensive Magic Show!" His voice was deep and gravelly. He bowed, then sneered some more and faced his audience again, standing on tiptoe.

"Here I stand, floating two inches off the ground, wearing my Incredibly Expensive Floating Shoes (only $249.99 while supplies last). I shall now perform my Incredibly Expensive Drop of Blood Trick ($174.99, knife included). Watch how I pierce my thumb with this blade. Yes, ladies and gents, it's a real knife. Watch me squeeze out a drop of my own blood! I press my thumb with my fingertip. One second, two seconds, release. *Wow!* What do we have here? Ladies and gents, the drop of blood has been transformed into a . . . ladybug!"

The Great Rob-o held up his hand. "Hold your applause, please! What's that, ma'am?" He listened patiently to a question from the imaginary audience. "Rest assured, ma'am. Neither the ladybug nor the Great Rob-o have been harmed during this Incredibly Expensive Trick."

Robert opened his top dresser drawer.

"And now, ladies and gents, it's time for the Incredibly Expensive Handkerchief Surprise (only $349.99, with a DVD and hand-woven silk handkerchief included)!"

Robert pulled a pair of his underpants from the drawer, stand-ins for the incredibly expensive hand-woven silk handkerchief. He turned the underpants inside out, then right side out again. "As you can see, there's nothing whatsoever inside this handkerchief," he assured his audience. "Now, sir, I wave the handkerchief around your head, like so, and, what's that you say, sir? There's a mouse in your lap? It must have magically appeared from inside the handkerchief! And now I will make that mouse disappear again!"

Robert stopped waving the underpants. Harry Houdini, who had been scampering around the room during the trick, *had* disappeared, but into the clothes closet. He found the mouse shivering inside a sneaker.

"Come here, fella," Robert whispered. He held the struggling mouse against his T-shirt and flopped down on the bed again. He could feel Harry's heart pitter-pattering.

Harry's accusing left eye looked right at him, reminding Robert of someone, but he just couldn't think who it was at that moment. He patted Harry's head until the mouse's long, ridged tail finally stopped twitching.

Green likes mice. Actually, when you came right down to it, he did. They were sort of like very small friends.

"Stay, little guy," Robert whispered. But now he could feel Harry's claws really digging in, so he let the mouse go. Harry scurried across his chest and under the bed again.

Robert sighed. He gathered up his tennis balls and tried to juggle again, but lacking the Gravity-Defying Juggling Balls, he failed miserably, as usual.

What a jerk he'd been, thinking he could tame and train his own mouse! And all those ladybugs he'd collected in the empty lot, none of them with any talent. Oh, how he wished he had big bucks so he could send away for those incredibly expensive tricks! Then he'd find out how they were really done.

"Those online videos tell you nothing! They just get you to shop!" he called out to Harry Houdini, whom he could hear scuttling around under the bed.

The truth was, he wasn't even sure Harry was a mouse. There was a chance he was a small rat. Maybe that had been the problem in the training department. And of course there would be no way to convince his mother to keep a rat.

Performing great magic tricks just wasn't in his future.

Except . . . except for the possibility of real magic.

On a night table by his bed was the book he'd borrowed from Ms. Snoops, *Incredible Magic Tricks for a Rainy Day.* Incredibly babyish tricks, thought Robert.

Except . . . except for that one trick—the one trick which cost $174.75 online, and according to the website had been a closely guarded secret for over one hundred years. But to Robert's amazement, there it was in *Incredible Magic Tricks for a Rainy Day,* for anyone to discover, whether it was raining outside or not—for free!

And Robert had the trick's magic ingredient, the ingredient that would guarantee the trick's success, safely tucked away in his backpack.

A car honked twice beneath his window. Robert grabbed his backpack and opened the window.

"I'll be right down, Dad!" he hollered.

That's when Harry Houdini sprinted across the bed, jumped onto the windowsill, and in an instant, poof!

Disappeared.

EVENING

Just Enough Time

It was evening on Orange Street and you could see the sun, like a juicy orange itself, slowly dropping down, down through the palms and the sycamores. As it dropped, you felt the air cooling your skin, at last. You breathed in the sharp supper smells—different smells from different windows: grilled cheese (301), turkey burgers (301 ½), salmon croquettes (302), scrambled eggs (303), franks and beans (305), teriyaki chicken (308), and more. If you stood smack in the middle of the block, all the smells jumbled together into one big spicy stew.

And you'd hear things you didn't hear during the day—

blaring TVs, a toilet's flush, a tired kid crying about one thing or another, an old bird squawking "All You Need Is Love."

Minutes before the sun went down completely, it was as if every single thing on Orange Street stopped. No smells, no shouts, no songs—everything as still as a photograph. Just that big old orange ball hanging in the sky, waiting to drop so that night could take over. You were waiting, too; waiting and watching, holding your breath those very last seconds, and then, (so quickly you missed it!) the sun splashed into the ocean and disappeared.

Evenings didn't last long. That particular evening, there was just enough time . . .

Just enough time for Harry Houdini to streak twelve times through the weeds and flowers and vines of the empty lot with his brother and two cousins, then follow his mother up the tree's trunk, hang out for a while, then race down again to gnaw on a fallen orange.

And for another mother to hover in the branches of that tree, making quick figure eights with tiny wings. Enough time to search with tiny diamond eyes, and know that something was missing.

And for Ruff and Mitzi to chow down, and then enjoy an evening game of fetch (Ruff) and one long, meticulous bath (Mitzi).

And just enough time for Bunny/Bonita to chat with her mom by phone, as she watched the sun go down over Orange Street. It was a sunset her mother had already seen, two hours earlier. There was enough time to scribble down a note: PLANE TOMORR. MORN., 10:33 A.M., TREE, and then think about her brave pioneer ancestors, Bunny and Augustus. Sure, they had lots of worries, lots of reasons to quake in their pioneer boots. But at least they didn't have to worry about the plain old sky over their heads.

And there was just enough time for Leandra to tell the truth.

Leandra, Big Mom, and Little Pop were sitting around the table in the Jasmine Pink living room section of her grandparents' home. In the center of the table was a small FedEx box. Inside the box was a dessert bowl lined with a soft nest of tissues, where Bean had been placed.

"Uh-huh," Big Mom was saying into her cell phone. "Uh-huh . . . Right. Excuse me . . ." Big Mom put her hand over the receiver. "Make a blanket with one of those tissues, too. Go ahead. Cover it up. It needs to be warm."

Gently, Leandra covered the bird with a tissue blanket. Maybe Bean would feel too warm, all covered up on a warm evening, or maybe not warm enough. You usually feel kind of shivery when you're not feeling well. Leandra herself did, anyway. Who knows how a speck of a hummingbird was feeling?

"Uh-huh," said Big Mom, continuing her phone conversation. "Well, too late now. Hmmm . . . Will do. Uh-huh, for sure! Thanks so much for returning our call, Carlotta."

"What did she tell you?" Leandra asked, when Big Mom had hung up. "Does it have a chance to live through the night?"

"Of course!" said Big Mom, bending over the dessert bowl. "Well, if we do our parts right, according to Carlotta. Very nice, smart gal. She said we could call her whenever we need to."

Carlotta was the wild bird expert, and Big Mom made it sound as if they were friends for life. "What are our parts?" Leandra asked.

"First of all, keep it warm. And offer it little drops of water, just as we've been doing . . . But she suggests using the tip of a toothpick instead of the sponge we've been using. It will take as much as it needs. Honey, go get some of your toothpicks from the pantry," Big Mom said to Little Pop. "And try to calm down that jealous parrot, will you? He's not fooling us for a minute." To get attention, Nelson was doing his famous impersonation of a boiling teakettle.

"Check," said Little Pop. He went across the big room to the Hot Banana cooking section of the apartment.

Leandra's mother came through the door, carrying a plate of brownies.

"How's it going?" she asked. She peeked into Bean's dessert bowl.

"Pretty good. But we'll have to stay up all night," said Big Mom, selecting a brownie.

"We'll do it in shifts!" said Leandra, happy to stay up all night. She'd always wanted to find out what that was like.

"Carlotta said you probably should have put it back in its nest right away," said Big Mom.

"But it looked like it needed nursing! Anyway, it's too late now," said Leandra. She glanced out the window at the darkening sky.

"That's what I told her," said Big Mom, "but first thing tomorrow, that's what you have to do."

Leandra didn't answer.

"I repeat," said Big Mom, "first thing tomorrow morning, that bird goes back to its mother where it belongs!"

Leandra's mother smiled. "It's not a pet, Leandra," she

said. She pulled Leandra onto her lap. Leandra still fit, but just barely, as she leaned against her mother's big, warm belly.

"And you'll have another baby to care for soon," said her mother.

"I know, I know," Leandra said.

"Can't find the toothpicks!" yelled Little Pop from across the room.

"Try the medicine cabinet!" Big Mom yelled back.

Leandra hugged her mother. It was true that she was always telling other people to grow up, but it sure felt good to be babyish occasionally. She felt a sudden kick from inside her mother, like a message from her baby sister. *Go on. Tell them.* Yes, it *was* a good time, Leandra decided, especially now that Little Pop was out of earshot.

"It's the giveths and taketh," she said.

"What?" asked her mother.

"That's why I've been so grumpy."

Big Mom leaned over. She put her big hand under Leandra's chin and turned Leandra's head so she was looking right at her. "Listen here," she said. "The Lord giveth and taketh away; we're born, we die. But one thing has nothing to do with the other. Understand? Nothing at all! Your grandpop will be here doing push-ups and revving up the battery when that baby arrives."

"OK. Just thought I'd mention it," Leandra said, as if those black-magic thoughts hadn't been bothering her at all.

"Here we are!" said Little Pop, returning with the box of toothpicks, another dessert bowl, this one filled with water, and Nelson, perched on top his head. "Nelson just wanted to see if we still loved him. A few peanuts should help, before he goes back into his cage."

Leandra could feel her heart expand inside her chest. It was a funny feeling, partly relief, and partly love, no doubt about it, even though she'd only known Bean for about four hours. And she could do her part real well, no doubt about *that*, either, for any other babies coming along. She knew that for sure now.

Or she'd known it for about two hundred and forty minutes.

She got off from her mother's lap, and dipped a toothpick into the bowl of water. Bean opened its beak and drank.

That evening there was just enough time for Ali to see her father cry. She had never seen her father cry before.

Adults cried differently than kids did. Their shoulders shook more, heaving up and down. They usually had a tissue on hand, ready to blow their noses in, or in her dad's case, a hanky. Her dad always carried hankies, which had to be laundered every week. Now Ali wondered if he did a lot of crying at the grocery store where he worked. Probably.

"Don't cry, Papa," she said, throwing her arms around his waist.

Silly, because she was crying, too. Maybe she and Manny shouldn't have told her parents about Edgar's words on the swing, get their hopes all up. Maybe it had been their imagination? Because Edgar wasn't saying anything now. *Nada!* Nothing. Zero. Zilch. Silent as her heart-shaped stone.

There he was, looking so solemn in his cute blue dinosaur PJs. Boy, did he ever used to love those PJs! "Tyrano-sore-is-rocks!" Edgar used to shout. But all he wanted to do now was hug his mama.

"*Mañana es otro día,*" said Manny.

"We know, we know," said Mrs. Garcia, shifting Edgar onto her other hip. "The doctor says, be patient, give it time. But—"

And then her shoulders began to heave up and down, too.

Now Ali felt angry. Tomorrow is another day! What's with all this time stuff from everyone? Tomorrow comes, and then another one and another one and another one, and nothing changes!

"Gotta go now, little guy," Manny said. He patted Mrs. Garcia's shoulder, then bent down to kiss Edgar's cheek.

"Edgar, say, 'bye-bye,'" said Mrs. Garcia. Edgar looked up at Manny, then buried his head in the crook of his mother's neck.

"*Gracias, gracias, Manuel,*" said Mr. Garcia, wrapping Manny in a bear hug.

"See you, Manny," Ali said, and hugged him, too.

She went into her bedroom. All her found treasures were spread out on a green plastic garbage bag on the floor beside her little desk. Jar lids, nails and screws, the doll's head, the piece of charred wood, the sock, the heart-shaped stone, and a tennis ball, a broken flowerpot, some buttons. She would never, ever know the true facts about all that past stuff. But it cheered her up, shuffling things around, filling in the holes in the stories on her own.

Still, what was the *purpose* of stories, really?

"If only, if only," she whispered.

Wouldn't it be great if you had the amazing power to fill in the holes of the *future*, and it could turn out any way you wanted it to? Just like that, *Eureka! Shazaam! Presto!*

"Oh, grow up," Ali said.

Her dad stopped by her open bedroom door. "Come. Come eat," he said. His eyes were still red. "*Mañana es otro día.*"

"I'm coming, Dad," she said.

She was going to bury that stone again tomorrow: put it right back where she'd found it.

And there was just enough time for Robert to make magic.

He and his father were at the Wok and Roll, a restaurant in the little strip mall at the end of Orange Street. Every Wednesday evening without fail, they had dinner together, and it was often that restaurant because Robert loved the all-you-can-eat sushi buffet and his dad loved the stir-fry.

They didn't have much to say to each other, lately. "How's school?" his father usually asked. But school was out now, so conversation was kind of slow, and Robert himself didn't know what to talk about. His dad seemed to have a million adult things on his mind. You could tell by that glazed look in his eyes. Did they used to talk a lot? Before? It was kind of hard to remember.

"Dad—"

His dad was concentrating on the bill, and didn't seem to hear him. He always checked bills carefully, especially now that he was more worried about money.

Robert was ready to wow him with his trick. He hoped that would perk things up.

The trick was called the Rice, Orange, and Checkers Mystery. Some rice was placed under a cover. Some checkers were placed under another cover. An orange was placed under a third cover. The magician waved his hands over the covers, and wonder of wonders, *poof!* When the covers were raised, *the three items had changed places!*

True, the online version involved giant-sized colorful checkers, ceramic covers, and a whole orange. The version in Ms. Snoops's *Incredible Magic Tricks for a Rainy Day* involved ordinary checkers, a small chunk of orange, and empty tuna fish cans. There was also a lot of flapping about of white napkins, which the online version didn't require. But so what? When the trick worked, it was still astonishing. The trouble was, after hours and hours of practice, only Robert and his mother had been astonished so far.

Last week he'd tried to perform the trick for his dad at the same restaurant, and had failed miserably. Robert had brought his backpack containing his checkers and empty tuna fish cans. Then, using his leftover rice from dinner, and a couple of the orange chunks always brought to the table after the meal, he performed the trick. Or, rather, he tried to perform it.

Robert tried and tried, but the Rice, Orange, and Checkers Mystery just didn't work. The rice had stuck to the cans, the oranges stuck to (and stained) the tablecloth, and the checkers had rolled onto the floor.

"Hey, old boy," his dad said, tousling Robert's hair. His father always called him "old boy" when he did something babyish. "Maybe you need a little more practice." Then his father apologized to the frowning waiter for his son's mess, as if Robert were a pipsqueak wearing a bib.

The real mystery was why it worked at home for his mother. Robert had written down a list, in order to analyze the situation:

<u>HOME</u>
– orange from tree across street
– rice from casserole of tuna, mushroom soup,
broccoli, and celery
– tuna fish cans
– checkers

<u>RESTAURANT</u>
– Wok and Roll orange
– side order of sticky rice
– tuna fish cans
– checkers

The answer had jumped right out at Robert. The orange! Tonight he would perform the trick for his dad, again, but this time he'd brought his own orange chunk, from one of the special oranges Ms. Snoops had given him. (Of course it could have been the magic of the rice in his mother's casserole, but unfortunately, Robert had gobbled up all the leftovers. And yes, yes, his mother was easily impressed, but the fact was, *the fact was,* the trick had worked!)

He was ready to try again. This time it would be different. He could just feel it.

"Dad?"

Robert's father held up a just–gimme–one–second finger as he signed the credit card receipt, then signaled the waiter that they were done. Robert noticed that there was a stain on his father's shirt collar, the same stain from the Wednesday before.

"OK!" said his dad, putting his pen in the breast pocket of his shirt. "Ready to go?"

"Dad, before we leave—" Robert hurriedly arranged his leftover rice, orange chunk, cans, and napkins on the table.

"Robert, not that trick, again! This is getting silly."

"I've been practicing and practicing. It won't take long."

"People are waiting for our table, old boy."

"Dad, *please*! I need you to watch this!"

He hadn't meant to yell. But all of a sudden the whole place got quiet and everyone was looking at their table. Even the hungry people who were lined up at the door craned their necks to see what was going on.

His face had reached Embarrassment Level Three (beet), for sure.

"Hey, Rob. It's OK," his father said. He reached out to put his hand on Robert's shoulder. "Don't worry. I'm watching."

He was. He really was. He was staring right into Robert's

eyes. Actually, now that he had his father's full attention, there was plenty Robert wanted to talk about! Girls, for starters. And laundry: Doesn't his dad wash his shirts anymore, for halibut's sake? And does he think about his son during the week? Is his dad lonely? Lots of stuff.

"Trust me. You are really going to like this," Robert said.

Checkers–Rice–Orange.

The napkins flapped. His hands moved. He hardly had to think about it. The whole thing took about one second.

Rice–Orange–Checkers. There.

Robert looked up. Had his father seen the magic?

"Wow, oh, wow," said his dad.

And there was just enough time for Ms. Snoops to finish up a scrambled egg sandwich and some sweet ambrosia, brew a tall glass of orange–raspberry–zinger tea, plop some ice cubes into a glass, hunt for her favorite fine–point ballpoint pen, drink her tea (now refreshingly cool), hunt for the pen again, which turned up beneath the papers on her desk, then lose herself in memories of other days and other evenings, long ago.

And just enough time for the mysterious stranger to lean against the front seat of his green car, parked at the corner of the street for the best sunset view, and open his birthday gift.

Peel it, actually.

"Tastes just as I remember it," he said to himself. Mostly sweet, but tart, like happiness and sadness mixed together.

NIGHT

Awakened

The deep quiet of the Los Angeles night drowned out the sirens, the shouts, the thudding of helicopters, and the whoosh of cars driving by. On that particular night on Orange Street, the stillness was so loud it was like a whisper in your ear. You leaned way, way out the window and drank in the cool desert air, wondering what woke you up. The orange tree, its fruit lit by the moon, caught your eye. And then, your ear.

If the Orange Tree Could Speak

I am the oldest living resident on Orange Street. I, alone, the Valencia, know everything about this street. A blue stone, a dug–up jar, a "ghost," an orange cone—these are bits and pieces of someone's story I could tell.

And if I could speak, I would tell you mine.

From the city of Valencia, Spain, hundreds of years ago, Spanish seafaring explorers brought my ancestral seeds to the New World. Columbus, Ponce de León, de Soto, they all loved the fruit of Valencia! Orange groves sprang up in the Caribbean and the Florida wilderness, and soon, around the missions of California. The *other* California gold, that's what my orange ancestors were called.

And once, long ago, before the malls were built and the freeways crisscrossed the area, I was one of six hundred Valencias standing in Mr. Stott's orange grove. Orange blossoms fluttered in the wind, like big sweet snowflakes. When the fruit ripened, you could smell it fifty miles away.

I am a Valencia. That means my fruit has a seed or two. All right, sometimes three or four, or more.

I remember hearing Mr. Stott complain, "My customers are much too busy to spit seeds—there's talk of a miracle orange, no seeds at all!"

We Valencias shivered at those words. Would those strange seedless orange trees replace us? We reminded one another that our fruit was the most delicious of all, seeds or no seeds.

That was the year the Santa Ana winds blew down from the hills, hotter and drier than ever.

"My water bills are sky-high!" complained old man Stott.

We shivered again. Would less thirsty crops, like avocados, say, or strawberries or crape myrtle trees replace us?

Then came a drought and things got worse! Aphids crawled among our drooping leaves. We suffered disease. Winter winds whipped through our branches, which nicked the fruit. We were frostbitten. Oranges withered and dropped.

"I've had it!" said Mr. Stott, who dreamed of wearing a tall hat to cover his bald spot, and fancy suits and shiny shoes, instead of overalls and boots.

Over the years, one by one, he began to rip out the Valencias, chopping the wood for cordwood, replacing the trees with a new crop. As a tribute to my fallen brethren, Mr. Stott named this street Orange. I say its true name is Street of Blossoms, Gone Forever.

And what was that new crop? Houses! A grove of houses. And, eventually, a fire station, a warehouse, a McDonald's, a strip mall, a school . . . I am the only orange tree remaining, saved by old man Stott's young neighbor, Ethel Finneymaker, who lived across the street.

"Mr. Stott, please, please, please let this tree live!" young Ethel had pleaded. She and her friend Gertrude liked to climb to my topmost branch and hang upside down from their bony knees.

When old man Stott died, Mrs. Stott sold this last little plot, which has had fourteen tenants and three owners over the years.

If I could speak, I would tell you everything. When I sense danger, I can only hope. Yet, truly, I am so grateful for the time, for all the moments of my long and fruitful life. I spend my daylight hours watching and counting and remembering:

Five marriage proposals under my branches. Two yeses, three nos.

One backyard wedding, another rained out.

Fifty-eight babies cooing beneath me.

Seventeen small graves scattered nearby: cats, a macaw, a puppy, turtles, and assorted fish.

Two hundred and fifty-three barbecues.

Nine lightning bolts that just missed me.

Two hundred and one balls that didn't.

Three fires on the property.

One thousand gallons of morning juice.

Two runaway girls whispering in sleeping bags.

Nine broken arms, three broken legs, five sprained wrists, seventy-three bruises.

And the countless poems and drawings I've inspired.

And the earthquake tremors (only one causing branches to crack).

And the morning sunrises, some more amazing than others.

And all the crawling, buzzing, pecking, swooping, chattering beings I've sheltered.

As the night air cools, I stop counting. Instead I think about all your stories buried deep in the clay soil, nourishing my tough, old roots.

Larry and Pug Tilley,
306 Orange Street

L arry and Pug were brothers, but if you happened to see them together on Orange Street in 1967, you wouldn't even think they were related. Not that they really hung out together. Larry could finish his homework in thirty minutes flat, which gave him plenty of time to race out the door and play ball with his friends. He was good at that.

His little brother, Pug, was mostly good at collecting rocks, drawing, and dreaming. Pug had a turned-up nose, so everyone called him Pug. "Slow" was something else that they called Pug, and "strange," too. (No one would use those names in front of Larry, of course, or they would have been punched out.)

Pug had an icy-blue stone, which he'd found on the beach in Santa Monica, and he was always taking it out of his pocket, holding it up to the sun. He said it brought him good luck because it was heart-shaped.

"It doesn't even look like a heart," Larry said.

But Pug said, "It only looks like a heart to the person who finds it. That's what makes it special."

The way Larry figured it, it was as if a giant hand threw a bunch of their parents' genes up into the air. When the genes landed, some of those genes became Larry, and some became Pug. It was all luck, and Pug's stone wasn't helping him much. Larry knew he'd gotten the better deal.

Larry was tall and speedy like his mom, Marisa. Pug got her red hair, except his mother's was long enough to sit on. But you hardly ever found Marisa just sitting around. She did everything speedily, including her cooking and cleaning. Sometimes the boys would come home from school and find her on her hands and knees, using orange halves to wash the kitchen floor, rocking back and forth with the beat from the kitchen radio, or her own singing. (Like Larry, her favorite group was The Beatles; her favorite song was "Santa Maria" because that was her hometown.) Only the nice, clean smell remained when the stickiness was washed off. She baked pies with tender crusts, and cakes with frosted pictures on top because she loved to draw, like Pug. She made lots of ambrosia, Larry's and Pug's favorite dessert—ambrosia made of oranges, coconut, and sugar, all layered together in a sugary glop. Everyone said it was the best around—even Ethel Finneymaker across the street, who gave Marisa Tilley the recipe. That's because Marisa used the sweetest oranges from the highest branches of the backyard tree, which, believe it or not, she could reach, with the help of her long fruit pole—except for one big orange at the very top.

"If I could just reach that one orange," she said, "you wouldn't believe the ambrosia I'd make! And all our wishes would come true."

Some of Larry's friends would laugh because his mother was taller than his dad.

"That's not the way it's s'posed to be!" they'd shout, and Larry would have to punch them out.

But his dad, Ralph Tilley, was strong, even though he was short and skinny. The dogs never threatened him on his long mail route; Mr. Tilley knew how to stare them down. Some of those dogs weren't as gentle as Larry's old dog, Cream. Ralph Tilley's muscular arms were good for reaching under a sink to fix a leak, or hammering nails in his backyard toolshed, or playing catch with his sons. He had blue eyes like Larry, which were handsome to look at, except when they were icy-blue like Pug's stone. That's what Mr. Tilley's eyes looked like when he was angry. He didn't get angry often, although he didn't like it much when Pug dropped the ball in a game of catch, or forgot to put "I" before "E," except after "C." And one time those eyes got icy-blue for something Larry wanted to do. Larry never forgot that.

It was late one Sunday afternoon in early spring, and the orange blossoms were still perfuming the backyard. Larry and his dad were playing catch, and Pug was leaning up against the trunk of the orange tree, drawing in a big pad with a stubby pencil. Every time he finished a picture, he'd tear it from the pad and lay it out on the ground, one of his many stones holding it down. He drew a small cloud that happened to look like an igloo; a fat beetle with pincers; Mitzi, the cat from across the street, lounging under the tree with old Cream. And then he drew Mrs. Tilley, resting for a bit on the back stairs, a sprig of bougainvillea in her hair, which Mr. Tilley had pinned there.

Mr. Tilley looked over at all of Pug's drawings, and laughed. Then he said what he always said. "Hey, artsy-fartsy, what's the point of drawing? It's a big waste of time when the real thing is right in front of your nose!"

Larry could see those drawings, too. *I can draw just as well!* he thought. *Even better!* He knew how good it felt to capture the shape of a beetle, its hard shell shaded just right on the page. Drawings said, *Look! You'll see things you've never noticed before, even if they're right in front of your nose.* Larry wished he could sit down beside Pug, with his own stubby pencil, right out there in the open, instead of hiding behind the bougainvillea bush. That's where he usually drew in secret. Every now and then, he'd even write a poem on the page, to go with the drawing. The poems were nothing fancy, just words he liked. Poems could be short, but still say a lot. He liked that about poems.

Does Cream dream? Is that what those noises mean???

—L.T., 1967

Of course, after he finished a drawing or a poem, Larry would crumple it up and throw it away. He could see no real purpose in drawing, and boys didn't write poems, his dad said.

That afternoon, in the backyard, he got a great idea, out of the blue. Larry decided to make comic strips, just like the ones in the newspaper, except they would be about the kids on Orange Street and all the stuff they did together. And his dad could make copies of it on the mimeograph machine down at the post office, and Larry could charge ten cents a copy. Making some money, that's what the *purpose* would be.

But when his dad saw him scribbling and drawing under the tree, his eyes got that icy-cold look, and he said, "You, too? I told you, that artsy-fartsy stuff is not what men do."

But men did go to war. Around that time, the U.S. was fighting a war in faraway Vietnam, and Mr. Tilley enlisted in the army.

"It's my chance to see the world," he said to Mrs. Tilley. "To fight for my country!"

And to Larry and Pug he said, "Vietnam's a beautiful place, boys, with rice paddies and emerald jungles and dragon fruit and flying frogs."

Larry got the feeling that Orange Street, with its gray mourning doves and cracked sidewalks and single citrus tree could never compete with that beautiful place.

One day their father hugged the dog, kissed everyone good-bye, and told his family not to worry when he was gone.

"I'm bringing my good-luck stone," he said. Pug had given him his heart-shaped stone, and Mr. Tilley looked like he believed in it almost as much as Pug did.

Their dad wrote that he'd volunteered to be a tunnel rat—a soldier who crawled into small spaces to flush out the enemy. It was one of the most dangerous jobs of the war. *"It's a good thing I'm not a big man,"* he wrote. *"I fit just fine in those tunnels. But don't worry. All I've met in a tunnel is one scared chicken!"*

Larry wrote to him about baseball and hot days and Cream's fleas. He didn't tell him that Mrs. Tilley went around looking sad all the time, her long hair unbrushed; that she was not doing much cleaning, or singing, or drawing with frosting anymore. He didn't tell him his dad had left a great big hole, like the hole in Larry's mouth when a tooth fell out, which he couldn't help touching with his tongue.

One day Pug drew a picture of their dad with his beard, before he shaved it off for the army, and his blue eyes, as warm as an L.A. sky in summer. And that's when Larry started drawing again, too. His pictures were of the four of them having a picnic under the orange tree, or sitting around the kitchen table, everybody ready to dig into a boysenberry pie or last summer's fruit preserved for cold-weather eating.

You could tell it was winter because there were raindrops at the window, and you'd know the kitchen smelled like oranges, because it always did.

His dad wrote that he'd saved someone's life. He wrote that his best friend had died. He wrote about the mud and the dark and the clattering helicopters and jungle heat. Sometimes, for weeks, he didn't write at all.

One afternoon Pug asked his mother, "How do you spell Vietnam, anyway?"

She told him it was spelled "Vietnam," not "Veitnam," as he'd written it. She told him how to spell other words, too, like "platoon" and "battalion" and "infantry." Then, after Pug had checked things over and over, because he really wanted to get it right, he put a bunch of drawings into an envelope and mailed them off to his father.

That's when Larry learned the most important thing about drawing, something he'd known, deep down, all along. Homemade pictures said, *This is home. Come back safe and* sound. *We love you and we are thinking about you every minute—* even if the artist didn't write down a single word.

To Larry's big surprise, Mr. Tilley had learned the same thing in the jungles of Vietnam. He didn't think those drawings were artsy–fartsy at all anymore.

"NOTHING here is as nice as those pictures," he wrote back. *"Keep them comin'! I miss you all like crazy! I'll be home real soon. I'm going to build a tree house for you guys. And, for your mom, I'll set up some raised beds for tomato plants and sunflowers. Oh, boy, can't wait to take you all to a Dodgers game!"*

So Larry drew, too, one picture after another, his initials marked at the bottom of each one. He hoped the drawings themselves would bring their dad home from Vietnam sooner.

That would be their dad's last letter. The family was told that Ralph Tilley found more than a chicken in those tunnels. He was hit by a piece of a booby trap while he was crawling through one of them. He didn't return from Vietnam, but their letters and those drawings did. They came back with their father's shaving stuff, his clothes, and Pug's blue stone. And Mr. Tilley's body was laid to rest in Los Angeles at a military funeral with horns blowing.

After a while, Pug got it into his head to pin up the

drawings in the toolshed. "I will leave them there forever," he said. He put his blue stone on a shelf in the shed, too.

"You are so dumb!" Larry said. "He's never coming home to see them. There's no *purpose* in doing that!"

Larry had never called Pug dumb before. But this was a dumbness that had nothing to do with being terrible at arithmetic and spelling, and the forgetting of simple things: This was a dumbness that had to do with not realizing everything had changed. But Pug just kept looking at those pictures in the toolshed, and crying. His mother cried, too. Larry was too angry to cry.

Other things made Larry angry, too. Their mother was singing again, but in a sad voice now. That's how Larry found out she didn't want to live on Orange Street anymore. Sure enough, one day Mrs. Tilley told her boys they were moving to Santa Maria to live with her parents.

But what made Larry angriest of all was Pug's blue stone. He thought that Pug was dumb to think it could bring good luck. And he was angry at his father for believing that, too, even though being angry at a dead person felt dumb.

The day before they moved to Santa Maria, it was so hot, you could fry an egg on the sidewalk. Not that they had time to test that out, with all the packing they had to do. Their dog, Cream, had decided to disappear, spooked by all the boxes. The boys had been calling for him all day, and that was really tough. But worst of all, it was Larry's birthday, and his mother, sweaty and exhausted from packing, had forgotten. Larry waited all day, thinking maybe she had a cake or a pie or a small gift, hidden away as a surprise. But no dice.

"Tell her," said Pug.

"Nah," said Larry. "Why should I tell my mother when it's her own son's birthday? And don't *you* tell, either!"

Sometimes it felt like he needed to keep finding more stuff to be angry about, just to feed the anger, like a fire burning inside of him.

It usually cooled off when it got dark, but the heat woke him up early the next morning, before dawn. Larry lay there for a while, getting angrier and angrier. Then he jumped out of bed. Barefoot and in his pajamas, Larry raced out to the backyard toolshed.

He took down the old preserve jar where his dad had kept his nails. Out went the nails, and into the jar went his father's last letter, as well as a poem Larry had wanted to send him. He grabbed a garden trowel and ran out to the backyard, where he buried that jar, holding all its dead promises.

Then he remembered the blue stone and went back to get it. Scraping the dirt with his bare hands, he plopped the stone into the same hole, then covered it up.

But Larry wasn't finished. He found his father's matches in the toolshed and began to burn up all the drawings, one by one. And before Larry could stop it, one corner of a drawing, a little ember, really, burst into a flame again. One split second is all it took! The flame leaped up, like a long tongue, to lick the polka dotted curtain high up at the little window. First the wall, then the whole shed was on fire! Larry stood frozen, staring at the flames, too terrified to move.

It was Pug who saved him, racing into the shed. Just as Larry could draw really well, Pug could run fast when he needed to. He yanked his brother out through the toolshed door, yelling, "Mom, anyone, please! Help us!"

Mrs. Tilley pulled out the garden hose and Larry and Pug ran back and forth with buckets of water. Flames began to spread to the dry weeds surrounding the shed. Someone must have called the fire station because soon the sirens were screaming down Orange Street. The shed and garden were hosed down with bigger hoses from the fire trucks.

As the sun slowly rose they got the fire under control at

last. Neighbors who had wandered into the yard to help or gawk returned to their homes. Larry, Pug, and Mrs. Tilley sank to the ground against the chain-link fence, exhausted.

"Who started it?" Mrs. Tilley finally asked.

Pug said, "It was an accident."

But Mrs. Tilley stared hard at Larry. Suddenly her face softened. "Yesterday was your birthday," she said softly. "I'm so sorry."

And that's when Larry began to cry. "It was me," he said. "I did it. I was burning the drawings."

His mother pulled him close, whispering, "I understand."

A few embers were still sizzling and fizzling around the trunk of the orange tree, where water from the hoses had pooled. It was as if the tree itself had willed the fire to go no further.

Enough.

Mrs. Tilley slowly got up and went to pick an orange from a lower branch. "This is your gift," she said, handing the orange to Larry. "I'm much too tired to climb to the top for the highest one, but believe me, *all* these oranges are special. Make yourself a birthday wish."

They sat down on the back stairs for the very last time, and Larry peeled the orange. Its sharp perfume made the air smell less smoky. He shared the juicy chunks with his mother and Pug, so that their wishes would come true, too. The orange tasted tart, but mostly sweet, because that's what hot summer days will do. Larry wished for happier times, for all of them. He felt happier already.

The moving van rumbled down Orange Street. After their belongings were loaded and Larry and Pug had yelled for Cream one more time, and he'd finally crawled out from his hiding place under the back porch, they all piled into their car and followed the van to Santa Maria.

The house on Orange Street was rented many times over, until years later, an earthquake shook its foundation. That's when they knocked down the house and what was left of the shed. Nobody ever built them up again.

Much later, Larry figured out a few things.

An orange could be a pretty good birthday gift.

A blue stone was just a blue stone, except when it helped you think about other things.

A poem could be written by anyone.

And Pug wasn't dumb when he looked at those pictures, remembering good times, hoping for more.

One day, years later, because Mrs. Tilley had died, Larry returned to Orange Street. He was now a tall, bald man with a beard and a green car. And except for his height, he looked just like his father.

FOR DAD
<u>AN ORANGE</u>

A Pear's not a Green
An Apple's not a Red
It's not a Yellow
But a Banana, instead.
But an Orange
is an Orange.
Why?

If you don't pick them
Those other fruits go brown.
Rot!
Fall down.
But an Orange
Stays orange
All those hot sunny days
Soaking up those orangey rays.
That's why.
L.T., 1968

MORNING, AGAIN

The Color Orange, Again

The back bone connected to the neck bone
The neck bone connected to the head bone
Now hear the word of the Lord!

Little Pop was doing his exercises. Nelson was squawking. It was a morning like all the others at 301½, except it
wasn't, because Leandra had stayed up a lot of the night to
greet it. She'd even witnessed the sun rising for the very
first time, as it floated up like a lazy balloon from behind
the hills. The other difference was Bean, whose life they
had saved. It was a wonderful thing, to save a life.

Ali stood outside Leandra's house, waiting to help her escort Bean back home to the orange tree. She peeked into the FedEx box. "I'm glad everything worked out. It doesn't matter who nursed the bird, as long as it survived. You did a super job, Leandra."

"Thank you," Leandra said. Then she yawned, because of all the sleep she'd missed.

Ali thought Leandra looked different, somehow: She seemed sweeter, with a new, serene smile.

The girls began walking down Orange Street, Leandra carrying the FedEx box, Ali thinking about the Girls Who Save Birds' Lives Club.

"I'm sure your wishing stone helped save Bean, too," said Leandra.

"Well, I don't," said Ali. "Wishing is babyish and dumb. You only wish when there's nothing else you can do, and you've kind of given up hope. I was thinking of burying it again, except it's so pretty."

"I think wishing *is* hoping," Leandra said. "What's wrong with hoping?"

Ali stopped in her tracks. "Leandra Jackson! That is absolutely the most incandescent, amazing thing I've ever heard anyone say."

"What's incandescent?" Leandra asked.

"Shining and clear. Brilliant. I will try to remember what you said, always." And all of a sudden, incandescently, Ali knew what else to say to her friend. "I think you're going to make a great older sibling."

"You do? Really?"

"I do. I really do."

Robert noticed the hummingbird parade as the girls passed beneath his window, although he didn't realize it was a hummingbird parade. He did wonder what was in *their* box, why they kept bending over it, and murmuring quietly. He went to get his own shoebox, which contained a few orange chunks, an empty tuna fish can, napkins, and some leftover restaurant rice balled up in plastic wrap.

It was time. He was ready. Ready to wow everyone— especially Ali—with the magic and wonder of his ancient trick.

He ran outside and followed them down the street toward the empty lot.

"The Girls Who Save Birds' Lives Club should take turns guarding the tree," Ali was saying, as the girls reached the lot. "We have to make sure the babies are safe, until they can fly on their own."

"Oh, don't worry, I can handle it," Leandra said. "It's my project and my bird, after all!"

"It's not *your* bird!" said Ali.

"Well, who else's then? OK, the mother hummingbird's, of course, but I think I should be the human in charge." Leandra's new, serene smile had disappeared.

"Well—" said Ali.

"And I don't like that name for our club, The Girls Who Save Birds' Lives Club. Whee-hoo! What a mouthful!"

"We can talk about it later," Ali said, grinning. She was actually relieved that the old, bossy Leandra was back!

Bunny/Bonita was coming down the street. She was finishing up her breakfast banana and trying hard to concentrate on her right-side-of-the-mouth chewing—for her mother's safety. The good part about right-side-of-the-mouth chewing was it took her mind off her mother's airplane, but only for a few seconds at a time. As soon as she stopped chewing, her mind went right back to her worry.

And there were Leandra and Ali with that baby humming-bird! Bunny/Bonita tapped her mother's gardening hat, then blinked rapidly three times. Then she checked her ticking watch. They better hurry up and put that baby back into its nest, so she'd have time for her good-luck wave. Only twenty minutes left before the plane was scheduled to fly by!

The strange thing was, and they talked about this later, none of them had thought much about the orange cone since the other morning. It had been sitting at the curb in front of the lot for twenty-four hours, blending right in with the rest of the Orange Street scenery. This morning it had even taken on a kind of innocent glow, the color of sunrise and juice. It was only when that brown truck drove up the street, rattling to a stop right behind the orange cone, that they began to worry again about the color orange.

Reporting a Murder, Again

A man hopped from the truck and moved the orange cone from the curb to the sidewalk. When Ms. Snoops saw that man and that truck, she knew what was going to happen, just as the orange cone had forewarned.

She dialed 9-1-1.

"I'd like to report a murder," she said, when the dispatcher answered.

That wasn't exactly true, she realized.

"Actually, it's an attempted murder I'm reporting."

That wasn't true, either.

"The murder hasn't been attempted yet, but it will be attempted any minute!" She was practically whispering now, even though the attemptee outside the window couldn't hear her.

There was silence at the other end of the phone line.

Probably looking me up on the computer, thought Ms. Snoops. *As usual . . .*

Ms. Snoops seemed to remember causing a ruckus the last few times she'd tried to report a murder, as if she herself were the criminal. People even accused her of "crying wolf"! Wolves had nothing to do with this crime.

And how could they, when all the wolves, well, actually coyotes, poor things, had disappeared from the area, too?

Finally the dispatcher asked, "Is this another Bird of Paradise?"

"No. Those have already disappeared. Extinct on Orange Street, you might say."

"Dying potato vine or sick night–blooming jasmine?"

"Gone, too, from neglect and abuse."

Ms. Snoops supposed it was all there, lit up on the computer screen: all the old cases she'd reported in the past, to no avail.

"Starving cactus? Sunburned azalea? Weeping willow?" asked the dispatcher.

"Excuse me, I've never reported *those*! And certainly not

a weeping willow. I don't remember one growing in this neighborhood," said Ms. Snoops indignantly. She wasn't sure, but she thought she heard the dispatcher giggling.

"Who, or what, is going to be murdered this time?"

"A tree. A very old orange tree."

"Whoa. I'll get the entire police force right on this."

"You're making fun of me."

"Ma'am, I have a hard job, sometimes a sad one, and yes, I'm not taking you seriously. Thanks for making me smile this morning, but I just can't tie up this line."

"I guess I understand," said Ms. Snoops. "I just didn't know who else to call."

Ms. Snoops hung up the phone and sat down on her orange and green striped couch, plucking at the antimacassars. Mitzi padded over and added a few snazzy scratches to the stripes.

"Well, I'm glad I made someone smile," she said to her cat.

That was one of Ms. Snoops's rules of life: Always try to make at least one person smile as you go about your day. It was a worthwhile rule, except it didn't feel as worthwhile when that person was smiling at your expense—or at the expense of a worthy cause, such as saving an old tree.

Ms. Snoops thought of another rule of life, one she was breaking that very moment.

Don't just sit there. Do something.

Do something about that huge brown monstrosity of a machine parked in front of the empty lot and its heartless, cigar-chomping driver at the controls, and his muscular helpers. She'd seen their likes before, on Orange Street. She knew what murderous crime they were contemplating. That orange tree had survived lightning, fires, and earthquakes, but it would never survive that vile crew!

But Ms. Snoops couldn't think of anything to do. She didn't feel like eating her breakfast, or drinking a last glass of fresh, organic orange juice (a heartbreaking thought), or walking across the room to work at her desk. It all felt so inevitable.

So Ms. Snoops just sat there breaking her rule for a few minutes. Then she decided to go to her desk and call 9-1-1.

"Madam," said the dispatcher, after Ms. Snoops had described the situation. "9-1-1 is not for garden emergencies, as someone has explained to you earlier this morning. Please don't call us again."

Ms. Snoops caught her breath. "Have I already called this morning?"

"Yes, dear. And yesterday morning, too. Maybe a little note near your phone would help."

"I am so, so sorry to keep bothering you," said Ms. Snoops. "I'm having a bit of a memory problem, lately . . . I promise it won't happen again."

Ms. Snoops peeled off a yellow Post-it note on which she drew a circle with 9-1-1 inside of it. She drew a thick, dark line across that circle and stuck the Post-it to the phone.

"Now, now, magic now," Ms. Snoops whispered.

Then she plopped herself down on her orange and green striped couch again and began to cry. She cried and cried until her chest ached. She cried for all the neglected plants that had died over the years, and for her disappearing memory and for one beloved tree and all its stories.

Gone, going, and about to be gone. Mitzi jumped onto her lap, licked a tear that had fallen onto Ms. Snoops's knuckle, then curled up for a nap.

"The only thing I can do," Ms. Snoops said, stroking her cat, "is dream the impossible." That was another rule of life that she tried to follow, from time to time.

Mitzi's tail quivered in her sleep, as if to say: If something's impossible, what's the point of dreaming about it?

"I know, I know. Cats dream only of possibilities, such as chicken and catnip," said Ms. Snoops, wiping her eyes on a sleeve of her bathrobe. "There's no point in dreaming the impossible. It just makes me feel better."

Ms. Snoops began to dream and imagine and wish for two impossible things.

First she wished she could go back in time.

She wished she were that same girl with bony knees, that girl who liked to look at the world upside down from tree limbs, with her best friend, Gertrude; that girl who, dizzy from the blossoms' perfume, made up stories, even before she got the idea to write them all down.

She wished she were that girl who learned to make ambrosia from her mother, who learned it from Mrs. Stott; that girl who believed Mrs. Stott when she said ambrosia was the food of the gods and made you immortal; that girl who had pleaded, "Mr. Stott, please, please, please let your orange tree live!" when old Mr. Stott bragged about his plans for a backyard swimming pool—and Mr. Stott said that he would consider her request.

Ms. Snoops wished she could go back in time, better yet, *stop time*, right on the morning of that very day, because that had been one of the happiest, amazing mornings of her life. She had been so relieved. Though old Mr. Stott died before the day of the planned backyard excavation, Ms. Snoops wanted to believe he would have honored her request.

Now Ms. Snoops dreamed and imagined and wished for the second impossibility, the craziest one of all: She imagined she was a main character in a book, or maybe even a Hollywood movie! Just around now she would do something important to save the day.

But I'm not a character in a book or a movie, thought Ms. Snoops. The day had come and she didn't know how to save it. This thought made Ms. Snoops leaping mad. That is to say, so angry she leaped up from her orange and green striped couch, sending Mitzi tumbling. She ran to the window and jerked it open.

"Hey, you! LEAVE THAT TREE ALONE!" hollered Ms. Snoops, shaking her fist at the driver of the brown truck. There went another of Ms. Snoops's rules: Always speak in modulated tones. But Ms. Snoops didn't care, because a rule of life may be broken for an important reason. And that was another rule of life.

The kids of Orange Street were standing in a knot at the edge of the empty lot. Startled, they all turned and looked up at her.

The Gruesome Details

L et's go back in time, but only a few minutes or so. Sid (according to the name embroidered on his shirt) had begun to relay the gruesome details of the killing to come. He thought the kids were interested in learning about his job.

"First thing you do is strip off all your smaller branches and limbs," Sid said calmly, his hands in his pockets. "Debranching, we call it."

Ali felt dizzy. *Debranching* sounded unsettling.

"Then, we feed the branches and limbs into that wood chipper over there." Sid, his hands still in his pockets, jerked his head toward a huge funnel on wheels, attached to the back of the truck, "That does the trick. A big mess of sawdust is what you get!"

It was clear those weren't gruesome details to Sid. They were just the ordinary details of Sid's job, in which he took great pride. It was easy to imagine him telling other kids those details, say, on Career Day at his son's or daughter's school.

"Then comes the stump grinder," Sid continued.

"The stump grinder?" whispered Bunny/Bonita. That sounded like something from a horrible, bone-chilling movie, the kind she wasn't allowed to watch. (Except for those trailers that popped up unavoidably, every now and then on TV.)

"Rocks the tree's stump back and forth to loosen 'er up," Sid said. "Then it's easy to dig the stump out, just like a big, fat molar."

The kids turned to the Valencia, looking as fresh and morning-pretty as ever, not like the condemned prisoner it really was. There was a silence, and for one whole minute, even if any of them had known the entire *Oxford English Dictionary* by heart, not one of the kids could think of a single word to say.

There was a peculiar smell to that moment: Sid's cigar

mixed with Ruff's fresh poop on the parkway (which Bunny/ Bonita quickly scooped into a bag), and oranges and musty leaves; or maybe it was the smell of sadness, or fear, if those feelings had a smell.

Ruff himself ran into the lot to curl up under the tree, as usual.

As Bunny/Bonita's watch clicked, suddenly the words returned, in the form of questions.

"Hey, what about all the oranges?" asked Robert.

Robert pictured the truck crushing all the fruit, then a great geyser of juice gushing up and splattering all over Orange Street, lost magic and opportunity disappearing down curbside drains, forever.

"Kid, oranges are a dime a dozen, or whatever the going rate is at the supermarket," Sid said with a not unkind, lopsided grin.

"You'll dismantle the swing for us, won't you?" asked Manny, who'd arrived with Edgar in his stroller.

Sid shrugged, as if dismantling a child's swing was a very, very minor problem. "Of course. We'll make sure you get it."

"What about the birdhouse? And the wind chimes?" asked Bunny/Bonita.

"The nests! What about the nests?" asked Ali. "You can't

see them, but believe me, there are nests there! Some are as small as walnuts."

Then Leandra whispered, "What about the babies?" She murmured something into her FedEx box, and that's when Robert realized she had been comforting something tiny and alive.

Robert also realized something else.

It was a terrible time for a magic show.

He could have a hundred, a thousand, a million bucks of incredible equipment in his shoebox. He could have, say, an elephant in there, an elephant just waiting to disappear into thin air! Even magic in the shape of some orange chunks and tuna fish cans! But all that wouldn't make a bit of difference. Manny was right. If your audience doesn't want to be wowed, there's just no magic there. *Incredible Magic Tricks for a Rainy Day* had neglected to tell him that.

"Whoa, wait a minute, kids," said Sid, holding up his hands as if they'd all been hurling eggs at him, instead of questions. "You'll get your belongings, and some oranges, too, if you like. The rest, I can't help you with."

"Is there anything we can do to save the tree at this point?" Manny asked. Edgar began to fuss in his stroller, as if he, too, recognized that something was very wrong.

"Sorry," said Sid. "The tree is on private property."

Bunny/Bonita glanced at her watch. There were ten more minutes to touch the sky.

Then Ali asked the question everyone had been thinking, but hadn't gotten around to asking: "Why are you doing this?"

"The owner—hey, there he is now—wants to clean up and level the land. He'll be building a house on the lot. He said something about wanting to say good-bye to the tree." Sid chuckled. "Imagine that . . . Saying good-bye to a tree!"

A green car was turning the corner, just around the time an amazing chain of events began to unfold on Orange Street.

An Amazing Chain of Events

That's when
Ms. Snoops leaned way out over her windowsill and
hollered, "Hey, you! LEAVE THAT TREE ALONE!"

Then
the kids of Orange Street turned to look up at her.

At that moment
the owner of the empty lot, Larry Tilley, got out of his
green car.

And it was at that moment—

not a moment you'd expect anyone to be pondering the meaning of words—that Ali suddenly realized the amazing complexity of the word "owner." She thought about how dollars and cents and deeds of sale and all those thick sheaves of paper Leandra's real estate agent mother made sure people signed, well, all that meant piddley-poo and diddley-squat.

"YES, YOU LEAVE *OUR* TREE ALONE!" she hollered at Sid, who blinked and took three steps backwards, as if she'd just turned on a wind machine.

And then

Bunny/Bonita, struck by her own sudden thought—a thought that took her breath away, concerning squirrels and hummingbirds and ladybugs and other living things that foraged for food for their families (which, when you came right down to it, were nature's equivalent of BUSINESS TRIPS!!!), all returning to find that their homes and families had *disappeared* off the face of the earth,

drew herself up as tall as she could, then gave the same brave shout as that wonderful pioneer woman of long, long ago, the original Bunny Perkins.

"AU-AU-AU-GUSTUS!" she hollered.

And Bunny, brave, formidable Bunny, forevermore Bunny,

her eyes smart and squinty in the morning sun, fearlessly kicked the orange cone out of her way as she streaked toward the orange tree, her purple hat falling to the ground behind her.

"Hey!" yelled Sid.

Then
Ali, admitting to herself that Bunny had just had an amazing idea, cried,
"You'll have to *debranch* the tree with all of us on it!"
And she followed Bunny.

As did Robert, for the oranges, and the possibility of real magic, and other reasons he wasn't quite sure about yet.

As did Leandra, for every single one of the babies—in a nest, inside a mother, in a swing or a stroller, or inside a FedEx box.

"Hey! Hey!" Sid continued yelling, and started after them.

But Bunny, so skilled at climbing this particular tree,

swiftly pulled herself up to a thick branch, straddled it with her legs, and continued pulling and straddling until she reached a high, thick limb on the south side. And Ali, and then Robert, settled on limbs below her. Then baby Bean was passed ever-so-carefully in its little lined dessert bowl from Leandra, up to Robert, up to Ali, up to Bunny, who placed it with its sibling into the nest as tiny as a walnut, on top of the Birdhouse of the Golden Arches.

Then they waited. Waited and hoped. Would the mother come? they wondered.

She did! She had been waiting, too. Twittering, the mother hummingbird darted to her babies and fed them with her long, pointed beak.

And Bunny, Ali, Robert, and Leandra watched, hardly breathing.

Then the unbelievable happened. Actually, several unbelievables:

Larry Tilley, his arms crossed at his chest, his blue eyes wide open, stood facing the children in the tree. He walked over to Sid and said something only he and Sid could hear. But everyone heard what Sid said, which was, "Are you kidding?"

Apparently Mr. Tilley wasn't, because Sid picked up his orange cone, hopped into his truck, started up the engine, and drove his lethal weaponry away.

There's a little break in the amazing chain of events here, because that's when time stopped. Well, that's what it felt like to the kids in the orange tree.

If joyful astonishment had a smell, it would smell like the perfumed air high up in that tree, among the most perfect oranges. The oranges hung like ornaments from old summers, great globes of hidden sweetness, touching the sky. So many things in the world seemed to be disappearing, so many sad, difficult things in life were impossible to stop, but, together they'd taken a stand (actually a *climb*) and stopped this one terrible thing from happening.

That's why they couldn't have been more astonished if they'd stopped time itself, which, of course, they hadn't, because at that moment, right on schedule, nobody noticed an airplane glinting across the ice-blue sky. Moments later, it would land, safely, without any help at all from Bunny.

And then

the amazing chain of events was set in motion again.

Robert loved being so high up in the tree. Looking down at the fence where the bougainvillea vine grew, he could see the five hidden ALIS he'd composed using seeds and twigs and petals, not counting the one Ali had already discovered. *What if she could see them, too?* he thought. *So what? Let her!* Hifflesnuffling wasn't a crime. And as long as he was way up there among the perfect oranges, Robert couldn't resist picking one of the oranges for a future magic show, when he'd have a more attentive audience. Then he picked one more, as a spare.

Just at that moment

Harry Houdini finished gnawing the stem of another perfect orange, at the very top of the tree, the biggest one of all, still hanging after who-knows-how-many years.

Purposefully targeted or not, that orange bounced off Robert's head and landed in his lap.

"OW!" cried Robert.

He looked up and recognized Harry. Robert knew it was Harry because if you spend an hour or so in close quarters with a rodent, you notice individual differences, compared to other rodents of your experience. Also, he realized why that particular rodent looked familiar. Harry had the accusing, critical gaze of Mr. Pokrass, the principal of Robert's school. Robert stared back defiantly, feeling happy and brave and not at all like an emotional lagger.

And that's when

Robert got his own amazing idea, although it didn't seem so amazing at the time. He had three perfect oranges in his lap. There was one dog and one person looking at him, needing to be wowed; he could just tell. It was as good a now as any to stay in, and try to juggle. He threw one orange up, caught it and—

"Hey, look at me! I'm juggling!" Robert shouted. He added the gift of a perfect shark face to his performance, just to spice things up a bit.

And one second later
that's when
Robert was beamed by another orange. (He'd always say it was Harry.)

And that's when (because there can never be too much joyful astonishment on any one morning)
Edgar laughed.

And

just before he fell from the tree, landing with a thud and breaking his arm in two places, Robert looked up to see Ali smiling, just for him. He could hear Ruff barking, and Edgar laughing and laughing and laughing, and something that sounded like a chorus of tiny angels, all the way down.

Ms. Snoops Remembers Again

More tea?" Ms. Snoops asked Larry Tilley. "Another chicken salad sandwich? How about some more ambrosia?"

Larry patted his stomach. "Couldn't eat another thing."

"Much healthier than hamburgers and fries!"

"Much healthier."

"Oh, it was so good to go back in time with you! I remember your house so well. The trim was painted chartreuse and the door was yellow. I remember Marisa's boysenberry pie. I remember Cream. And the boys! Does Pug still like to draw?"

"He does," answered Larry.

"And how is young Larry?" Ms. Snoops asked.

Larry paused. He put his hand on Ms. Snoops's cheek, as soft as crushed velvet. "He's fine, Ethel," he said.

"Good. I am so glad you visited, Ralph. When you go home, make sure you kiss Marisa and the boys for me," said Ms. Snoops.

It has been such a nice morning, she thought, even though the details were fading quickly; only the feeling was left. But it was a peaceful feeling, the kind you get when a story is ending.

AND

Other Days

Let's say you were a stranger, visiting Orange Street, after all of this happened.

Maybe you'd wonder why three girls and a boy (two of the girls with very short hair, the other with dreadlocks) met regularly under that orange tree in the empty lot. You'd notice that kids from nearby blocks would join them every now and then.

What were they all arguing about? Everything: their next letter to the president, for example; whose turn it was to weed and fertilize; how much admission to charge for the Great Rob-o's Incredible Magic Show; and to which worthy cause he should donate the money. And they weren't arguing, as Rob-o said in an e-mail to his old friend Nick. They were having a loud *discourse* (*dis´kors, v. to talk*). Occasionally one of the kids would sprawl under the tree, or perch on a big branch, to read, or write, or draw, or just to think about this or that . . .

(Nick e-mailed back, saying he missed his former street and former continent. And he missed Robert, of course.)

And you'd probably be curious to know why the owner of the empty lot wasn't developing it just yet, and what it was that the elderly woman was reading to the group. And what all that digging was about.

And then there'd be that business with names.

You wouldn't understand why Leandra called her baby sister "Bean."

Or why, for that matter, Bunny was Bunny. And why she waved at an airplane from the orange tree, every now and then, if she had the time.

And maybe you'd wonder why Robert, long after his broken arm had healed, kept a frayed "Best Wishes for a Speedy Recovery" in his pocket, which he pulled out to look at, every now and then. Or why Ali had drawn a tiny heart over the "I" of her name, when she'd signed that card. (She often drew that heart, but sometimes she didn't. The point was, that time she did.)

And you'd probably be surprised to see Ali and her friends high–fiving one another, when she showed them the following note from her brother Edgar's preschool teacher:

Edgar is sometimes a tad too boisterous and doesn't stop talking to his table neighbors. But all in all, coming along nicely.

You wouldn't understand any of this, unless, of course, someone explained it to you, or wrote about it in their memoirs or in a story.

The kids of Orange Street always remembered that morning when everything connected in the glowing moments of the Magic Now, like juice and pips and pith inside the skin of an orange. When all that really mattered was an old tree, a baby bird in its nest, and a little boy's laugh.

They would look for those moments all of their lives. And they would find them.

Ethel Finneymaker's Ambrosia

- Slice your sweetest oranges.
- Layer dried coconut and sugar in between them.
- Let the whole thing sit for a while, so all the tastes come together, infrangibly.
- If you feel especially celebratory, add some whipped cream.

Enjoy!

AUTHOR'S NOTE

The orange industry thrived in Southern California for many years, and oranges have been called the other California gold. The Washington Navel, referred to in my story as a "miracle" orange without seeds, did, indeed, supplant most of the Valencia variety. Other industries, as well as suburban development, diminished the orange industry itself, but every now and then you will come across a beautiful, bounteous old Valencia in someone's backyard, including my own.

My tree inspired this story, as I began to ponder how the past can inform and inspire the future, and how the precious moments of the present connect us with every living thing. I imagined an orange tree growing in an empty lot—a space "empty" of structures and residents, but filled with neighborhood children, animals, insects, and plants. The lot contains many layers of history, both literal and figurative, as my character Ali discovers, digging in the dirt. I was moved to write two specific stories which represent two layers of that history, and also reflect achingly familiar modern issues.

Gertrude and Ethel are children growing up during the Great Depression, a worldwide depression of the 1930s during which many people suffered the hardships of unemployment and severe poverty. There was great economic disparity; Ethel's family is much more financially stable than Gertrude's. Gertrude and her parents are from Oklahoma, a region where many farms were devastated by dust storms and drought during that period. Thousands of families migrated west, looking for work picking crops in the huge, fertile agricultural fields of California. But wages were very low and conditions in the migrant camps often unbearable, as described in my story. Gertrude is left with distant relatives, and though deprived of affection, she is at least guaranteed regular meals and schooling.

In 1941, the United States entered World War II. Many warships were needed. Gertrude's parents are hired by a shipyard in Richmond, a city in Northern California, and Gertrude is happily reunited with them.

Young Larry's story takes place in 1967 during the Vietnam War, a complicated conflict between communist North

Vietnam and the government of South Vietnam. The United States supported its anti-communist ally South Vietnam, hoping to prevent totalitarian domination of all of Southeast Asia. It was a long and deadly war. American advisors were first sent to the region in the 1950s; the war ended in 1975 with the capture of Saigon in South Vietnam by the North Vietnamese army. More than 58,000 U.S. soldiers and millions of Vietnamese were killed in the conflict.

During the time in which my story is set, men were drafted into the army. (Women did not fill active combat roles in those days.) Because he has a family to support, Mr. Tilley is not drafted. He enlists on his own to serve his country.

ACKNOWLEDGMENTS

My deepest thanks to Will Wardowski, PhD, Professor Emeritus of Citrus Studies, University of Florida, for his careful reading of my manuscript and for leading me to John McPhee's wonderful book *Oranges*. The PLGA and Sontag Foundations were invaluable for my understanding of cerebellar mutism, and Elizabeth Partridge's *Restless Spirit: The Life and Work of Dorothea Lange* allowed me to "see" Gertrude's world. To my editor, Maggie Lehrman, and my agent, Erin Murphy, thank you for your amazing guidance. And a huge thank-you to my family; you know what you did.

And Sophie Beglinger, in your swing, as well as your family, you have been an inspiration.

ABOUT THE AUTHOR

JOANNE ROCKLIN is the critically acclaimed author of several books, including *Strudel Stories*, which was a *School Library Journal* Best Book of the Year and an *American Library Association* Notable Book, and *For Your Eyes Only!*, which was a *School Library Journal* Best Book and a Bank Street Best Book. She lives in Oakland, California.

This book was designed by Maria T. Middleton and art directed by Chad W. Beckerman. The text is set in 13-point FF Atma Serif, a modern typeface that incorporates transitional elements similar to those found in Baskerville. FF Atma Serif was designed by Alan Dague-Greene in 2001 for the FontFont type foundry.

The interior illustrations were drawn in pencil by Chris Buzelli.